Strange Case of
Mr. Bodkin
and
Father Whitechapel

the other side of Robert Louis Stevenson's
Strange Case of Dr. Jekyll and Mr. Hyde

M. Elias Keller

STRANGE CASE OF MR. BODKIN AND FATHER WHITECHAPEL
COPYRIGHT © 2012 BY M. ELIAS KELLER
ISBN 978-0-615-67024-9
PRINTED IN THE UNITED STATES OF AMERICA

COVER PHOTOGRAPH: Amanda Stevenson Lupke

GZI PRODUCTIONS EDITION
FIRST PRINTING: 2012

STRANGE CASE OF
MR. BODKIN AND FATHER WHITECHAPEL
M. ELIAS KELLER

A brilliant reinvention of Robert Louis Stevenson's *Dr. Jekyll and Mr. Hyde*—published with the full original classic in a flip edition.

"Had I approached my discovery in a more noble spirit, had I risked the experiment while under the empire of generous or pious aspirations, all must have been otherwise, and I would have come forth an angel instead of a fiend..."

Published in 1886, the tale of kindly Dr. Jekyll inventing a potion that releases his repressed persona, the evil Mr. Hyde, is one of the world's best-known stories. But Jekyll's turn for the worse was only the beginning. Shortly after the doctor's untimely death, his estate is sold to cold-blooded banker Geoffrey Bodkin, who stumbles upon the fateful potion and unleashes his own alter-ego: Father Whitechapel, saintly almsgiver to the East End paupers. But what begins as a story of loving charity soon becomes one of embezzlement, scandal and murder, as Mr. Bodkin struggles to keep Father Whitechapel from being branded London's most notorious villain—Jack the Ripper. Keller masterfully evokes Victorian London and its vernacular in this suspenseful debut novel, taking literary adaptations to a new level of sophistication and virtuosity while exploring timeless themes of class warfare, the dark side of philanthropy, and the catastrophic consequences of unhindered goodness.

"An innovative and fascinating literary venture"
Independent Publisher

A London Book Festival 2012 Selection

INCLUDES READING GROUP GUIDE

CONTENTS

Author's Preface

That night I had come to the fatal cross-roads. Had I approached my discovery in a more noble spirit, had I risked the experiment while under the empire of generous or pious aspirations, all must have been otherwise, and from these agonies of death and birth, I would have come forth an angel instead of a fiend. The drug had no discriminating action; it was neither diabolical nor divine; it but shook the doors of the prison-house of my disposition; and like the captives of Philippi, that which stood within ran forth.

—*from* Henry Jekyll's Full Statement of the Case

Since 1886, when Robert Louis Stevenson first published *Strange Case of Dr. Jekyll and Mr. Hyde*, the "Jekyll and Hyde" split personality has become part of our collective mythology, as shown by countless adaptations of the tale, on page, screen and stage. But I do not believe there has yet been a re-telling of *Dr. Jekyll and Mr. Hyde* that presents the *other* side of the story: the saintly outcome of quaffing the potion. With *Mr. Bodkin and Father Whitechapel*, I have intended to do just that: bring forth the angel instead of the fiend.

Although *Mr. Bodkin and Father Whitechapel* is, of course, fiction, many of the story elements were inspired from factual history and most of the newspaper excerpts are taken near-verbatim from their sources. The Charity Organisation Society and its vehement critics are quite real, as was (Sir) Charles Stewart Loch, whose personal diaries I was fortunate to obtain from the Senate House Library of the University of London. Several other characters are real people, too, including Rose Millett, an East End prostitute who met an untimely death rather similar to that in my story.

Mr. Bodkin and Father Whitechapel is a fully self-contained tale, but I have published it in tandem with the original *Dr. Jekyll and Mr. Hyde* to encourage readers to experience both stories, in whichever order they prefer. Most everyone knows the Jekyll and Hyde story, but not nearly as many have read the actual novella, which besides being an astonishing feat of concision at only 26,000 words, remains ingeniously constructed and thoroughly suspenseful to the very last sentence. It has been an unexpected pleasure to become so intimately acquainted with this masterpiece, and I hope that *Mr. Bodkin and Father Whitechapel* pays due homage.

MEK
PHILADELPHIA, 2012

STRANGE CASE OF
MR. BODKIN
AND
FATHER WHITECHAPEL

OBITUARY.

HENRY JEKYLL, M.D., D.C.L., L.L.D., F.R.S., aged 48, physician and scientist of London, died on the eighteenth of March in his home, from a sudden and undiagnosed illness. Colleague of the late Dr. Hastie Lanyon, Dr. Jekyll was educated at Eton and Cambridge as a Medical Doctor. He began his career on the medical faculty of the University of Cambridge, where he distinguished himself for highly original scientific theories and laboratory experimentation. Throughout his career, Dr. Jekyll tended London's eminent citizens as well as offering his expertise to the indigent; he held many public appointments and memberships in professional and social organisations, and was foremost in all good and charitable works. He died unmarried; private interment; funeral arrangements by Gabriel J. Utterson, Esq.

Meeting at the Bank

ST. JAMES—To be SOLD, the LEASE of a first-class MANSION, attached, in fashionable neighbourhood, fit for immediate occupation. The accommodation comprises 14 bed and dressing rooms, four rooms on the first floor, three rooms on ground floor, capital offices, handsome reception rooms, grand hall and staircase; good stabling. Elaborately fitted throughout with great taste and latest improvements; modern drainage. Large private cabinet with facilities suited to a medical gentleman. For terms and cards to view apply to G. J. Utterson, 9, Gaunt Street, as above. *The Times.* September 6, 1888.

DESPITE THE COMFORTABLE ATMOSPHERE and elegant décor of the office suite, often spoken of as the pleasantest room at Coutts's bank, Mr. Utterson the lawyer felt a shudder in his blood. His otherwise rugged countenance testified to some deep-seated terror of the mind, as though from a recent shock, and from the present gloom of his spirits, he seemed to read a menace in the fine furniture and costly cabinets of oak, the rich curtains and posh carpets of many plies and agreeable in colour, the gleaming mahogany table and commode-on-legs, and especially the imposing desk, behind which sat the noted banker and financier, Mr. Geoffrey Bodkin, a rugged, thick-set, pock-faced man of forty-odd years; plain but fashionable in his dress, and sedate in his deportment.

"There is some mistake, it seems," Mr. Utterson stammered, as he caught up the paper on which the banker had written his bid. "The property is worth twice that, sir—easily so."

"Pardon me, but I have researched the house quite extensively," the banker began, "and a large section of it is a medical laboratory. You will find few buyers that have both a need for such apparatus and the wherewithal for such a home. Therefore, the new owner must expend a significant sum to revert that back to a proper garden. This clearly affects the value."

"I am aware of that," Mr. Utterson rasped, flushing at the mention of the laboratory; "and the listed price reflects as much."

Mr. Bodkin waved a meaty hand at the real estate listing. "Perhaps, at one time, this was a fair price," he replied cuttingly. "But I will point out that there was some scandal surrounding Jekyll's death, which has caused others to shy away from the property, and which further weakens the value."

"I do not know what you refer to," returned the lawyer, a good deal offended by the other's speech, and now affirming for himself what the banking world had long known: that insofar as business dealings were concerned, Mr. Bodkin was the most cold-blooded animal London ever produced.

The banker snarled aloud into a savage laugh. "As you like. But I do not think that anyone else has made a serious bid on the property?" Mr. Utterson grunted in acknowledgement;

and Bodkin continued icily: "And I also believe that Jekyll's entire estate was bequeathed to you alone—nearly a quarter-million sterling, it was? I should think that would be windfall enough to avoid this silly haggling."

"Sir," returned Mr. Utterson, his voice harsh and broken, "that is really not fitting language. I assure you that I am far from seeking to profit from a friend's death. Know, too, that the estate will be put to building a new hospital, in Jekyll's name."

For all the force of Bodkin's cowing, the last was spoken with a strangling anguish that caused the banker to draw back momentarily. "Well—that is a commendable endeavour," he answered. "But it does not alter the matter at hand. Whatever the proceeds of the sale, it *is*, in fact, pure profit on your end. Isn't it most expedient to accept a reasonable offer and be done with the whole affair? You plan to leave London shortly, do you not?"

"Yes, I am going to live abroad," Mr. Utterson answered, embarrassed by this line of discourse. "Jekyll's death was—a great blow to me."

Mr. Bodkin slid over the contract he had prepared beforehand. "Well, then, sir," he said in a slithery tone, "if this is all that keeps you in London, why quibble over numbers like some costermonger? Come, be a gentleman, and be done with it already."

Mr. Utterson rose from his chair and stepped away from the desk, making a feint of going to the water-pitcher. After a step or two, however, he paused, putting his hand to his wetted brow like a man in mental perplexity. Even among the shrewd, hard-driving businessmen he often encountered in his work, Bodkin seemed a step beyond; Mr. Utterson could think of no living thing, save one, that he had ever regarded with as much disgust and loathing. "Good God," thought the lawyer, "is this even a man? Like some damned money-grubbing Juggernaut."

Mr. Utterson hesitated for another moment; but then, as if upon some sudden recollection, fronted about with an air of resignation, and the two men stared at each other pretty fixedly for a few seconds. "So be it," the lawyer murmured, "it shall be over."

Shortly thereafter, when the papers were completed, Mr. Bodkin turned to a small cabinet behind his desk. "A drink to mark the sale? This is a very rare vintage."

"No, thank you," Mr. Utterson answered, limply accepting Bodkin's handclasp. "I must be off."

And with that, the enfeebled lawyer departed, ashamed at this disagreeable transaction, yet relieved to be gone from the bank, and from Mr. Bodkin, and indeed, to be speeding away from London, forever.

CHARITY ORGANISATION SOCIETY.
Central Office—15, BUCKINGHAM ST., ADELPHI, W.C.

PATRON—THE QUEEN.
PRESIDENT—THE LORD BISHOP OF LONDON.
CHAIRMAN OF COUNCIL—THE LORD ABERDARE
TREASURER—G. BODKIN, ESQ.

N.B.—No direct applications for Relief can be received at the Central Office.

MODE OF OPERATION.

Each committee establishes an Office to be a centre of charitable organisation in its District. The inhabitants of the District, WHETHER SUBSCRIBERS OR NOT, are invited to refer to the Committee all cases of need and indigence requiring investigation, and are supplied, on request, with tickets bearing the address of the Office. If requested to do so, it communicates the result of such investigation to the person desiring inquiry, and should he wish to undertake the case, leaves it in his hands. In the absence of such wish, the Committees deal with each case to the best of their judgment and ability. District Visitors, Dispensaries, and Hospitals are invited to refer cases requiring investigation to the Committees.

Wayfarers and vagrants, if they appear to be in extreme want, have bread given them **TO BE EATEN AT THE OFFICES**, and receive such advice and assistance as the circumstances of each case require. The public are therefore earnestly requested **NOT** to give direct relief to applicants in the streets.

The Society desires in every way to promote personal intercourse between different classes, and they invite all willing to assist them by visiting, or in other ways, to send in their names to the Office of their District, or to the Central Office of the Society, at 15, Buckingham Street, Adelphi. They earnestly deprecate the supposition that the committees, if supplied with money, will be able to do all the work of individual charity. They wish to make their Offices centres of local information, to encourage judicious work of all kinds amongst the poor, and to get many more persons to assist in doing it.

The Reports of the Metropolitan Charities and numerous Books of Reference on Charity and the Poor Law can be seen at 15, Buckingham Street. Members of District committees and the public generally are invited to consult them there; or to write to the Secretaries for information on any practical points contained in them.

The Charity Organisation Reporter, published weekly during Sittings of Council, is sent post-free for a year for 5s.

CONTRIBUTIONS for the work of the Society are earnestly requested, and may be paid at the Central Office, 15, Buckingham Street, Adelphi; or to the account of the Charity Organisation Society, at COUTTS & Co.'s, 59, Strand, W.C. Contributions for the poorer District Committees can be paid to the "District Committee Aid Fund" of the Council.

C. S. LOCH, Secretary.

The Secretary

CHARLES STEWART LOCH, SECRETARY of the Charity Organisation Society, was a man of stringent disposition never lightened by sentiment: brusque, austere, backward in ideology, and yet somehow regarded as one of London's leading men of philanthropy. He wrote prolifically, lectured widely, served on Royal Commissions as a prominent authority on the condition of the poor, and throughout England was known simply as "Loch of the C.O.S.," for he himself was the embodiment of his organisation's principles and methodology, whereby thorough investigations were made on the conduct, character and capability of applicants, and relief given only on the pretence of self-dependence and permanent benefit. "The answer to the old question," he used to say, sternly, "is that Cain and Abel are each their own keepers." And indeed, Loch was sincere; his beliefs echoed loudly from the set of honourable principles that guided his life. Few men could read the rolls of their life with less apprehension than Mr. Loch: never had there been a whiff of personal scandal about him; he was circumscribed at worst, shunned vintages and spirits, cared well for his family, and adhered to his own rigid standards of thrift and prudence.

For all that, his organisation, far from being esteemed, was roundly condemned: Loch and his cronies were labelled miserable doctrinaires; judgmental, prying, hard-hearted, and stingy; mocking rather than helping the poor. It was inevitable that he would run counter to others and be criticised in his lifetime; yet Mr. Loch pressed on indefatigably to propagate his principles of wise charity, not to be swayed by the shifting winds of trends or the epithets hurled toward his life's work. And at council meetings, propounding in the company of friendly colleagues, something eminently humane beaconed from the secretary's voice; his call for sober, judicious charity, for providence and virtue on the part of the indigent, for a renewed fellowship between rich and poor, for widespread agreement that to build up self-respect in men and women was the greatest charity of all, seemed reasonable, even wise. "Not alms, but a friend"—this was his guiding principle, the spirit with which he endeavoured to imbue his Society and create of its workers and volunteers an inspiring force for preaching and practicing personal service, and those who had the opportunity to see Mr. Loch at work could scarcely disagree that his life was full of unselfish toil and utter devotion to his cause.

This morning, as Mr. Loch was reviewing his correspondence at the Society's Central Office, which made its home on a peaceful street running to the old Water Gate of York House, he was interrupted by a soft knock at his door, and his undersecretary announced one Mr. Snell. Mr. Loch bid entry, and a moment later entered Harry Snell, a young investigator of the Society. This village boy from Nottinghamshire was one of Loch's most favoured workers: inclined by nature to industry, frugal and sparing as to personal expenditure, of likeable disposition and lucid in communication; and therefore it was to the secretary's great surprise, and manifest disappointment, when the young man announced that he was quitting the Charity Organisation Society.

"But why?" returned Mr. Loch. "Your work has been quite good."

Snell bowed his head briefly in gratitude. "Thank you, sir, but I have had an extraordinary experience, an epiphany, even, and now I want to do a different type of work."

Hearing this, Mr. Loch suddenly noticed the change in the young man's appearance. Gone was Snell's expression of methodical briskness; he seemed intoxicated, his eyes injected with newfound mysticism. "Come, Harry, this is all very abrupt," the secretary said. "Speak to me, tell me what has happened, and perhaps there is some solution."

After a moment's hesitation, the young man began his tale: "A few days ago, I was coming home from Whitechapel, off Mile-End Road, I believe it was, quite late at night. The family I had been trying to visit was never in during the day, and I finally went in the dead of the night to determine whether they actually lived at that address. Well, my way lay through a courtyard where there was literally nothing to be seen but the most indecent and distasteful. Street after street, and all the windows broken out and stuffed with rags—street after street, all mucked up like a sewer and foul as a privy—till at last I got into that state of mind when a man begins to wonder just what God means by allowing such hellish quarters.

"Then all at once I heard a patter of footsteps. I expected to see the usual, a policeman and his bull's eye prodding along some vagabonds—but instead, I saw a lone, tall figure gliding along eastward at a good pace, and a crowd of maybe eight or ten stumping along behind. Well, sir, it was a sight to see: this man, erect and snowy-white, dressed very plainly, but strolling with exceptional grace, and the flock of tramps, their clothes rags and feet bursting from the sides of their shoes, clustered round and gazing up at him as though he were the second coming. It sounds nothing to hear, but it was heavenly to see. I took a liking to him at first sight; and slipping back into the shadows, I trailed the gentleman and his adoring throng for a while. No matter how grimy or tousled a child approached him, no matter how coarse a man pawed at him for a coin, no matter how lewdly a fallen woman beckoned, no matter how bedraggled a stray animal crossed his path, he kept perfectly poised and uttered no reproach, but only gave a look of such compassion that it brought tears to my eyes. It wasn't like a man; it was like some blessed angel. The people who had turned out to see this figure greeted him like his own family, the women weeping at the sight, and pretty soon the figure began taking from his satchel coins and provisions and passing them round, at which point the crowd became so tightly packed about him that it was hard to see where one person ended and another began.

"But most affecting was when this gentleman encountered a small girl whom they call Margates, poor and dejected, a half-witted orphan, they say, not more than eleven or twelve, alone in the street, for God knows what reason and subject to unimaginable indignities. Well, the child was shoeless and one could plainly see the festering sores on her feet. And what do you think that strange figure did? —but sat right down on the kerb with the poor girl, doctored her feet with his hand-kerchief and some liniment, then produced a pair of shoes from his satchel and slipped them on her feet. She flung her-self into his lap and sobbed; he cradled her for a minute, tears streaming down his own cheeks. I followed him for another hour or so, as he entered various tenements and lodging houses, or tended to people on the street, until finally, I lost track of the gentleman in that maze of winding alleys."

"Tut-tut," said Mr. Loch. "One of those slum saviours, engaged in precisely the type of charity that does more harm than good."

"I thought you'd think so, sir," answered Snell. "But if you had seen what I did, you'd realise that my man was one that would be difficult to condemn, a really saintly man, one of your fellows who truly does what they call good. Well, perhaps it's as they say: God is where the poor live," he added, and with the words, fell into a vein of musing.

From this he was recalled by Mr. Loch asking rather suddenly: "And you feel that such promiscuous charity as that truly helps the poor?"

"Well, sir, that's not for me to say," was the reply. "We mean well enough, but I am beginning to hesitate at putting questions to the poor. It partakes too much of the style of the day of judgment. A more Christian rule, I wonder, would be that the more it looks like aid is needed, the less to ask."

"A very perilous rule, too," said Mr. Loch, disapprovingly. "From my own bitter experience, be assured that this man's hand will close after the first novelty of distress wears off."

"I am not so sure about that, sir," Snell relayed, with deep feeling. "There is something different about this man, something unexplainable. If there is a good beyond the good our Society strives to reach—I daresay that man has reached it. Never have I looked upon anything that so confirmed my love and trust in the Almighty, and so made me question my own purpose."

Mr. Loch frowned behind his ponderous moustache, which concealed both his top and bottom lips. "Well, I cannot speak to that," he finally said. "There's one point I want to ask, though. I want to ask the name of the man who gives the handouts."

"I can't be exact on that point," admitted Snell. "No one seems to know his name. He goes only by 'Father White-chapel.'"

"Hm," said Mr. Loch. "What sort of a man is he to see?"

Snell pondered for a moment, but then shook his head. "He is not easy to describe. There is something uncanny with his appearance, something inordinately pleasing and down-right angelic. I never saw a man so appealing, and yet I can name nothing out of the way. He's an extraordinary looking man, and yet I really couldn't specify the point. No, sir, I can't describe him. And it's not want of memory, for I declare I can see him this moment."

Mr. Loch ruminated on this while rising to his feet. "Well, Harry," he said, looking down his beak-like nose at his former employee, "every man is entitled to, and responsible for, his own decisions. I sincerely hope that you are making a wise one. As it is, I must return to my work."

"I am sorry, sir," Mr. Snell murmured, accepting the hand-shake of the secretary. "I do not mean to trouble you."

"It is not myself that you should trouble over," Mr. Loch returned grimly, bearing the full brunt of his authority upon the young man; "but rather the sake of London."

"A CAUTION."

It appears there is a new East-End Salvationist practising indiscriminate charity, who goes by the moniker of "Father Whitechapel." May I, through the hospitality of your columns, beg this person to refrain from encouraging unemployed men and wayward women to take up a life of vagrancy and begging? This he can do simply by withholding the coppers and silver at present so easily forthcoming as a sop to conscience or as the result of a generous, but misguided, impulse.

There are no such robbers of the deserving as those habitual mendicants, given way to laziness, sloth and drink, who by false tales of distress divert into their own pockets the relief that is intended for real sufferers. This is the kind of rascality that the C.O.S. aims to expose and halt, and yet our task is all the more difficult in the face of rampant street charity, which disorganises charity and puts a bounty on its most transient and least noble impulses.

It is better to give constant support to an institution in which we have a personal interest than to help a large number by doles given in the street. Sixpence dropped into the hand of a beggar by a wealthy man may stand for the guinea that on fuller consideration he might have sent to the hospital direct. Yet there are large classes of persons who appear to resent the idea of applying principles of any kind to philanthropy. Almsgiving is for them a kind of moral self-indulgence which they like to enjoy when they feel disposed, but are unwilling to discipline with rules and guidelines, like a child slapping at a piano without learning to read music.

There is, unfortunately, a tendency to look askance at the Charity Organisation Society and its methods. People cry out for us to "Spend more! Give more!" But what they fail to realise is that it is all too easy to spend other people's money; and that contributors to our Society would be ill-treated if their monies were simply scattered among London's poor without conducting proper investigations into what this money will be used for and why it is needed in the first place. For those who misunderstand our methods, for those who confound true distress with mere aspiration for wealth and luxury, let them begin tossing money about the East End and see for themselves the evil effect of ill-advised charity. Money so given is usually much worse than wasted, for it tends to render helpless those who stand in need of industry, thrift, and above all self help, and therefore intensifies the distress it was intended to remove.

Indeed, those of us in England who were fortunate to be born to easier circumstances sincerely sympathise with the severe toil and self-denial which the poor's lot imposes. We also desire to tell them that we are ready to help if proper occasion should arise; and that if man, or wife, or child should be stricken with protracted sickness, or with some special infirmity, there are those who will gladly minister to his necessities, and do their best to mitigate suffering. But it is a hurtful misuse of money to spend it in assisting the labouring classes to meet emergencies which they should themselves have anticipated and provided for.

Those who will not concentrate charity will dissipate and waste it; those who will not investigate each case of homelessness will make vagrants; and those who will merely add more shelters will only make more burrows for the shiftless to slip into and disappear, rather than be caught and reformed. Only the most careful administration of charity can lead us out of darkest England. This involves hearing the stories of those in distress, visiting them, inquiring about them, planning how to help them to help *themselves*, raising funds to aid them, joining with others for their assistance—the daily and costly duties of the Charity Organisation Society.

Will Father Whitechapel, or any of your readers, volunteer for this desperately needed work?

I am, Sir, your obedient servant,

C.S. LOCH, *Secretary*

Charity Organisation Society

Story of the Door

ANONYMOUS DONATION.—The Reverend Samuel Barnett (vicar) begs to extend his deepest gratitude to the anonymous benefactor who has presented a munificent gift of £1,000 to the CLERGY DISTRESS FUND, which is being raised for the betterment of the Whitechapel district. *The Times.* October 13, 1888.

FOR SOME TIME NOW it had been a weekly tradition for Mr. Loch to whip up the circulation by way of a pleasant constitutional with Reverend Barnett, clergyman and social reformer of the East End. These two men, while claiming similar missions and enjoying each other's counsel, nevertheless differed on the principles of charity, and it was well known about town that the clergyman had long been at odds with what he considered the Society's over-careful philanthropy. Yet Mr. Loch was a model of courtesy; a quarrel never ensued; and perhaps as a testament to the regimented life of the secretary, the pair's regular excursions continued uninterrupted.

The morning was fine and clear, cloudless overhead, wet under foot with dew, full of chirrupings and sweet with autumn odours. Today's route led the two men through that citadel of finance, St. James Square, and down a small, quiet street, which instantly caught and pleased the eye of the passenger with its freshly-painted shutters, well-polished brasses, general cleanliness and gaiety of note. Their conversation began on small matters and niceties, though in short time the secretary's recent opinion-piece arose, and with it, the looming issue of Father Whitechapel.

"Someone would do well to tell him that his work is deeply flawed," Mr. Loch sighed. "Coins given in the street do little except to keep the destitute just there."

"Yes, I know you think so," Reverend Barnett said. "But take heed, Charles, not to condemn what you ought to woo. This Father Whitechapel has made quite an impression in the East End. Indeed, my parishioners hardly speak of anything else."

"That is usually the case," Mr. Loch parried, "with a nine days' wonder."

The reverend smiled wanly. "That I understand; and I suppose it must remain there," he answered. "However, Charles, since we have touched upon this subject, there is something I should like to tell you. I scarce know what to think about it, and you would judge wisely, I am sure." The reverend paused meaningfully, and then continued: "I suppose you read in the paper of that anonymous gift?"

"Oh?" Mr. Loch said, with sudden perspicacity. "That was from Father Whitechapel? But if that be so, why the anonymity, when already no one knows who he is?"

After a moment of reflection, the reverend replied, his tone dropped low. "That is a fair question, Charles, but between ourselves, the circumstances of that gift are connected to an odd story."

"Indeed?" said Mr. Loch. "And what was that?"

"It was this way," the reverend opened. "I was out for a walk, not far from here, in fact, and very early in the morning, just as the sunrise began to peek through the fog. Suddenly I noticed a strange figure crossing the roadway towards me. He was tall and very plainly dressed, but the look of him, even at that distance, was quite prepossessing. I had heard much of this Father Whitechapel, but never had I seen him. Yet something told me that this was him. I gently accosted him and introduced myself, mentioning the distress fund and my mission in Whitechapel, my motive being that he might volunteer to work with my parish—although something about his manner and the whole mystery surrounding him made such a thing seem out of the question. And indeed, he said as much, but that was not the end of it. 'Perhaps the next best thing, brother,' he offered. 'What shall it be? Name your figure.'

"Well, I was rather flustered at this, and I will say, too, Charles, that it was he, not I, who screwed the number up so high—it took some effort on my part to keep him at that—but at last he struck. 'Ay, brother, it shall be done,' he said, as easily as though agreeing to a shilling. Now, however, I was pushed to wonder if the offer was a serious one, and if so, the next question was how to get the money. But here is where it became rather odd. Father Whitechapel suddenly whipped out a key and slipped into a nearby doorway, and presently came back with a cheque for the pledged amount at Coutts's bank, drawn payable to the bearer and signed with a name that I can't mention—but it is a name that is rather well known and not one that is normally associated with such magnanimity. Yet the signature was good for that pledge, and much more than that, if genuine. It was a ticklish situation, but my benefactor gave another warming smile. 'Set your mind at rest, brother,' says he, 'and place your trust in those who would help you.'

"Indeed, the man seemed so pure and good, that I could no more cast aspersions than I could trample a child, and so I merely bid him my gratitude. 'With pleasure, brother,' he replied, 'though if you please, charity shall not vault itself, nor shall it profit me.' And with that, he re-entered the doorway and disappeared inside. I have not seen him since."

"One would suspect the cheque to be a forgery," Mr. Loch said, after some cogitation. "But it seems not."

"I gave it in myself the moment the bank opened," Barnett answered. "As good as gold. Now, what does a man make of such a thing?"

The pair walked on again for a while in silence, rounding a corner into a square of ancient, handsome houses, now for the most part decayed from their high estate and let in flats and chambers to all sorts and conditions of men: map-engravers, architects, shady lawyers, and the agents of obscure enterprises.

"Samuel," spoke Mr. Loch, "that's quite a tale of yours."

"Indeed, it is."

"However," the secretary resumed, "I should be careful accepting such gifts, lest you trade the good name of your mission for its prosperity. You and I well know that a man does not, in real life, walk into a place at the crack of dawn and come out with another man's cheque for a thousand pounds."

"True enough," the reverend returned. "But then again, people are in great need, and far be it for the Clergy Fund to deny such generosity."

"Still, it looks a bit like Queer Street, wouldn't you say?" pressed Mr. Loch, "or the dodge of some confidence-man.

That is my guess, though even that, you know, is far from explaining all." Barnett kept silent to this remark, and the secretary continued: "And you never asked about the place with the door?"

"No, but it is a curious thing," answered the other, and here, as the pair came abreast of a by-street, the reverend lifted up his cane and pointed across to the other side, where two doors down from the corner, on the left hand going east, the line was broken by the entry of a court, and just at that point, a certain cryptic block of building thrust forward its gable on the street. It was two storeys high and showed no window; nothing but a door on the lower storey and a blind forehead of discoloured wall on the upper. "There it is, in fact. It looks sordid enough now, and even worse in the dark."

Surprised out of himself, Mr. Loch gave a jerk that nearly threw him from his balance. He grew pale to the very lips; his shoulders drooped; and his breath came in short gasps.

"My dear sir," asked the reverend, "are you unwell?"

"Quite all right," Loch wheezed, pounding at his chest. "Just the old asthma."

"Well, anyway," Barnett continued, eyeing his companion warily; "it seems scarcely a house. There are three windows looking on the court on the first floor, none below; the windows are always shut but they're clean. And then there is a chimney which is generally smoking, so somebody must live there. Yet it's not so sure, for the buildings are so packed together about the court."

"Most curious," Mr. Loch croaked.

Thereafter, the two men wound back toward the main thoroughfare, with Mr. Loch absorbed in a deep silence and obviously under a weight of consideration. "Charles," the reverend said, with a touch of remorse, "I think you might have warned me, if you know more than you say." Mr. Loch sighed deeply but said never a word, and the reverend presently resumed. "Well, here is another lesson that silence is golden. I did not wish to cause trouble for this good man. Let us make a bargain never to refer to this again."

"If you insist, Samuel," returned Mr. Loch, as they parted ways, "I give you my word."

Mr. Loch Was Quite Uneasy

TO THE EDITOR OF THE TIMES.

Sir,—I wish to add my voice to the many who have foolishly donated money to Loch's C.O.S. and quickly felt the deep hypocrisy of these men. For in fact the reason for the existence of this society consists in that it acts as a buffer between the rich and the poor. Suppose a man with an income of £1,000 wished to give as little as he can for charitable purpose. Instead of devoting a tithe, the society says to him, "Give us £10, and we will find you with an excuse for not giving any more, so you will keep a clear conscience and pocket £90."

The principles of the C.O.S. are not according to the spirit of Christianity, nor the manly and generous character of Englishmen. If he saw a poor person in a gutter, he should give him a penny out of his own two-pence, without asking whether he was deserving or not. Yet this society mainly consists of idle rich people, too stupid, selfish, or lazy to expend their own money, and paid officials, wholly unfamiliar with the needs, necessities, and struggles of the poor. These people assume a social and mental superiority over the lower classes, lack the consciousness of collective sin, and most of all, are incapable of realising that wealth is a mere accident, and that failure, in a large proportion of cases, is also an accident. There have been instances of a respectable working-man being refused help for his starving family because records showed that twenty years previously he had been convicted of stealing a loaf of bread.

I should think that the true spirit of giving is in that beloved character of Father Whitechapel. Would the *Times* please print a means by which we might donate to his mission? My cheque-book stands ready.

I am yours truly,

O.V. MORGAN, Charity Protection League

I T WAS MR. LOCH'S CUSTOM of Sunday afternoons to enjoy time with his wife and children, often visiting one of London's public gardens or indulging in one of his personal pastimes of botany, law-reading, or water-colour. On this day, however, with Reverend Barnett's story resounding in his thoughts, Mr. Loch discharged other interests and duties to close himself in his private study, where he took from his Society files a sealed folio entitled "TREASURER'S REPORT: ADDENDUM," prepared by Geoffrey Bodkin, Esq.

This folio, the contents of which the secretary now studied with clouded brow, contained a memorandum that had been personally submitted by Bodkin and circulated at the last council meeting. It proposed a dramatic reduction of administration expenses, "by which a guinea is spent to give a shilling, and which inclines one to think that indiscriminate charity, much as it is to be deprecated, may yet be preferable." Besides that, the addendum called for an unprecedented centralisation and redistribution of Society funds, "such that our

poorest districts—namely, Spitalfields and especially Whitechapel—receive the funding so desperately needed."

The suggestion had incited considerable uproar; it was re-
minded, with some insistence, that operating costs were fixed,
and besides, the council had already established a means by
which the citizens of London could themselves donate to
improve the lopsidedness in district funding.

"Pardon me, Mr. Bodkin," an elder council-member named
Mr. Thornton had called out, loudly and without waiting for
acknowledgement; "we are not running a workhouse, and if
we will not expend the proper funds to maintain the dignity
of our Society, then it is not one to which I shall be subscrib-
ing."

There was a swell of "Ayes" at this comment; then came
the voice of another council member, Dr. Yates: "I suppose
you would have us do without offices or clerks? Perhaps we
should empty the bins ourselves?"—and here he received a
hearty laugh.

At this point, Mr. Harrison the barrister rose and addressed the high-ceilinged room with his flowing voice.
"Steady, gentlemen," he said to the room; and then, turning to
address Mr. Bodkin directly: "My good sir, perhaps it seems
like there is waste in our expenditures. But surely you agree
that it is well worth spending twelve shillings to ensure that
the other eight given will be well-used, rather than giving all
twenty to be squandered on shameful merrymaking?"

"Hear, hear!" several men called out.

"And another point," Harrison continued, in a rich, rolling
oratory, "regarding the unequal funding for our districts. Recall, sir, that we have already established our District Aid
Fund. That, to me, seems sufficient; I for one will not abide
the brunt of my own contributions being poured into that

festering swamp of Whitechapel. Relief must go to the most worthy, the most likely to re-enter the civilised world—not merely the most destitute; and certainly not just to the most horrid, depraved animals that come begging for food."

Mr. Loch, embarrassed for his friend, calmed the ruffled council and quickly tabled the matter; and no more was it mentioned. Yet the episode continued to haunt the secretary. Bodkin was an old mate and long treasurer of the Society; the very pink of proprieties; careful of his health and still more so of his reputation. Yet now he seemed under some new influence; else why should the hitherto aloof banker suddenly show such concern for the troubled Whitechapel district? Never before had the stodgy fiduciary voiced dissent; it was quite erratic for him to suddenly propose such a radical overhaul and, withal, draw attention to a persistent controversy.

Settling into his armchair, Loch now brooded in greater understanding and yet greater anxiety. It was one thing, the secretary thought, for Father Whitechapel to curry favour with London's residuum, but quite another to be slipping like a fiend into that seldom-used side door of Bodkin's house, and emerging with a hefty cheque signed by that tight-fisted banker. It offended Loch both as the public face of the Society and as a believer of sane, methodical charity, to which the impulsive was destructive. And his ignorance thus far of Bodkin's clandestine connexion with such a man as Father Whitechapel further swelled Loch's indignation. Bad enough that this imprudent naïf was rushing about the city tossing money to every moaning mendicant, irrespective of conduct or character. It was worse when the detestable ideology of blanket charity began to infect his own council, and now in Loch's mind there leaped up the sudden, definite presentiment of danger.

"Has all London gone mad?" the secretary wondered, as he replaced the obnoxious papers in the folio. "Perhaps Meade knows something more," he then thought, putting on a greatcoat and setting forth to Mayfair to see his old friend, Mr. Wallace Meade, owner and operator of the Meade Clothing Company, one of London's larger clothing manufacturers and what is commonly called a sweat-shop. It was a nut to crack for many, what these two men could see in each other, or what subject they could find in common, one being dedicated to assisting the poor, and the other known for grinding their faces. Yet these two were old school-mates both at Trinity and Balliol, and their affection and interest in each other, like ivy, was the growth of time, even if agreement in opinions did not always follow.

At Meade's home, Mr. Loch was admitted and subjected to no stage of delay; the spindly butler ushered him direct from the door to the dining-room, where Mr. Meade sat alone over a bottle of particular old gin, of which he was much a connoisseur. This was a hearty, healthy, dapper, red-faced man, with a shock of greyish-red hair and an outspoken and decided manner. At the sight of Mr. Loch, he rose up from his chair and offered a firm handclasp.

"Not come soliciting, have you?" Mr. Meade asked, with one of his characteristic guffaws.

"No, sir," Mr. Loch replied, forcing a thin smile. "I have well given up that chase."

"Well, it's nothing against you, Charles," said the other, as the two men settled into their seats. "But then I never went in for charity and the like. What is it, anyway, except more spent at the public-houses and rat-pits?" Mr. Meade harrumphed, rapping the arm of his chair. "The best form of charity, I say, is a sound economy. Everything else," he added, flushing crimson, "is wasted money or self-serving balderdash!"

This little spirit of temper was somewhat of an affront to Mr. Loch, but being a man inured to criticism, he merely nodded stoically. "Perhaps so, Wallace, but a sound economy is built on liveable wages."

Meade snorted, swirled his glass, and continued pontificating along a familiar line. "There will always be hunger, Charles. That is a fact of life. Natural selection and so forth. Some men thrive, and some go to the wall. I pay the wages that the market will bear."

"Starvation wages, you mean," Mr. Loch rejoined mildly.

"Starvation, sir, is a discipline," Meade came back with; "and London's poor would do well to have more of it."

This venomous comment silenced the room for a moment, as the once-inseparable pair looked upon the changed faces of each other and pondered the passing of time. "Be that as it may," Mr. Loch remarked, leading up to the subject which so disagreeably preoccupied his mind; "some men of business have done well for themselves with philanthropy. Take Bodkin, for instance."

Mr. Meade took from his glass and sniffed. "Yes, it does serve him well, seeing that half your council are already his clients, and his sights set on the rest."

"There may be some truth to that," conceded Loch, twisting at his side-whiskers. "And speaking of Bodkin, do you see him much these days?"

"I see him now and then," returned the other. "He advises on some of my investments."

"And I don't suppose," resumed Mr. Loch, musingly, "that he has ever mentioned a new acquaintance of his, known as Father Whitechapel?"

"Whitechapel?" repeated Meade. "No. Never heard of anything like that. Can't imagine any sensible bloke going near that hellhole, anyway, except for one thing, which is hardly fit to discuss." The merchant guffawed, but seeing Mr. Loch's stony façade, he continued soberly: "Indeed, Charles, I haven't heard anything about a new friend of Bodkin's. Certainly not with that name. Besides, Bodkin's dearest friend is his own purse."

That was the amount of information that Mr. Loch carried with him as he departed from Meade's house and set out for his own. The scud had banked over the moon, and it was now dark like the back-end of evening, save for the lamps, unshaken by any wind, drawing a regular pattern of light and shadow. London hummed solemnly all around; the fog slept on the wing above the drowned city, and through the muffle and smother of these fallen clouds, the procession of the town's life was still rolling in through the great arteries with a sound as of a mighty wind.

Hitherto the problem of Father Whitechapel had touched the secretary on the intellectual side alone, but now, traversing narrow labyrinths of the great lamp-lighted city, his imagination also was engaged, or rather enslaved. Like a scroll of lighted pictures, Mr. Loch envisioned the figure of a man gliding swiftly through decrepit alleys and doss-houses; then of a horde of loafers emerging from their burrows, drunk as lords; and then these met, and that human dole reward them with coins and provisions. And never did that figure halt: he would glide all night, more stealthily and more swiftly, and ever more swiftly, even to dizziness, and at every street-corner fill the pockets of a thriftless tramp.

Later that evening, Mr. Loch sat on one side of his own hearth, with Mrs. Loch upon the other, at a nicely calculated distance from the fire, and midway between them, the tea-things ready at the sitters' elbows. It was their habit of evenings to read together, either from a work of dry divinity or classical poetry, but tonight the volumes sat closed as Mr. Loch, the picture of bleary disquietude, stared silently into the flames.

"Charles, I think you might be worrying needlessly," Mrs. Loch began. "You have never heeded spiteful letters from ignorant people. Why now?"

Mr. Loch glanced over at his wife and smiled weakly. "I have said this before, my dear, and I will say it again. It is not that I am taking personal offense. But I worry for London. This frenzy in the East End will end badly, no doubt." He sipped from his teacup and nodded toward the stack of newspapers. "And it is unfortunate that by telling the truth, I am practically branded a heretic."

"I should think, Charles," said she, "that there is enough suffering in the East End for both your Society and Father Whitechapel."

The secretary looked over at his wife in surprise. "I wonder about you, Sophie, that still you do not understand the proper principles of charity."

"I wonder about *you*, Charles," Mrs. Loch answered, an angered pink in her cheek, "that those principles so completely overtake your heart, and perhaps your good judgment." Her husband did not reply; then, she continued: "I am sorry, but I too read the paper and I hear many things about Father Whitechapel. The man has clearly dazzled that entire district."

Mr. Loch shook his head sadly. "It is not the man they love, my dear, but the money he passes out."

"You may well be right, Charles, but either way, we must all pick our battles, and this may not be one worth waging."

To this Mr. Loch made no reply for some minutes, merely staring ahead to the fireplace, where the last log was quickly being engulfed and turned to ash. "Thank you, my dear; I believe you are only looking after me, perhaps better than I am looking after myself; but when this man's mania finally subsides and his purse is empty, those he now, as you say, 'dazzles,' will only be worse off."

Then, bidding his wife good-night, Mr. Loch went to his study to resume his moping. In the murky waters of the day's revelations and unresolved questions, his imagination was again piqued. He saw a vision of a room in a rich house, where his friend Mr. Bodkin lay asleep, and then the door of that room would be opened, the curtains of the bed plucked apart, the sleeper recalled, and lo! there would stand by his side a figure able, by some mesmerising charisma, to bilk away the earnings of his friend, and indeed all London's industry, to be scattered insensately among the city's undeserving loafers.

If he could but once prevail upon Father Whitechapel and explain the danger of his open-handed charity, thought Mr. Loch, it might diminish and perhaps roll away, as was the habit of unenlightened views when confronted with granite reason. If not, at least Loch might see a reason for Bodkin's strange preference (or bondage) that prompted the ugly addendum to the treasurer's report, and the large cheque to the clergy fund.

Thus it was that there sprang up and grew apace in the secretary's mind a singularly strong, almost inordinate curiosity to meet in the flesh this person. It would, at minimum, be a face worth seeing: the face of a man with infinite mercy, a face which had but to show itself to raise up, in the mind of young Snell as well as the pious Barnett, and indeed all of London, a spirit of enduring reverence that bordered on idolatry.

But how was Father Whitechapel to be reached? How persuaded? He, Loch, was too well known in Bodkin's neighbourhood to be lurking about the side-door and laying in wait; and yet he had no more specific destination to reach the ghostly almsgiver. Such was the problem that Mr. Loch set himself to solve, as he lay on his great, dark bed, tossing to and fro, and groping in all corners of his mind for any kindling spark that might light his way.

The Applicant

ROSE MILLETT, female, 29.
Applicant applied at Whitechapel district office. She lives in a common lodging house in George-street. Previously worked for Mr. Meade as a buttonhole maker but quit because of low pay and bone pain. Claims a child living under guardianship in Surrey, and assistance needed for school-tuition, but would not give detail for school to be contacted. Applicant said she recently had been helped by Father Whitechapel and spent nights in his room when she could not pay her rent, and he could vouch for her character. From further inquires it was found that the applicant goes by various names: "Rose" at times, "Catherine" at others; one girl who lives in the adjacent room said, "Oh, you mean Drunken Lizzie." Neighbours report that applicant is more often drunk than sober and goes out "hopping" to Poplar every night. Last year was sentenced to five days' imprisonment for public drunkenness and lewd behaviour. Her mother, Mrs. Margaret Millett, widow, of Pelham-street, stated that her daughter had been married but the husband had deserted her and fled to Ireland. Mother has not been in steady contact with applicant since about six years ago and had no idea

how her daughter was getting her living. Applicant expressed interest in mangle to get laundry work, but this is likely worthless given the numerous mangles already in the area. Very much given to intemperance and sin. *Not likely to benefit from relief.*

EARLY NEXT MORNING, MR. LOCH visited the Society's Whitechapel district office, ostensibly on normal rounds of business, but with an eye on learning more of Father Whitechapel. He was scarcely disappointed: his investigators had indeed heard much of this elusive do-gooder, for the masses of Whitechapel had taken quite a fancy to him, and in consequence, were growing ever more impatient with the Society's meticulous inquiries and systematised relief. Loch even listened as his volunteers lamented being spat upon by children and, amazingly, threatened with bodily harm by poker-wielding women. Yet when he fished for more specific information on the mysterious benefactor, none of his workers could confess to any personal encounters, and the bits offered seemed the stuff of legend.

"He walks with a little black book, I've heard," whispered Miss Reed, an investigator. "A book full of names, of people to be saved."

"And he is never seen during the day?" Mr. Loch pressed.

"Never," she confirmed fancifully. "They say he vanishes in the morning, with the stars."

Mr. Loch raised his eyebrows at the woman's story. "Take no mind of such foolishness," advised he, "and keep to task. I will see about this Father Whitechapel."

Here the secretary went to meet with the undersecretary of that district office and asked if any recent applicants had listed the mythical creature as a reference.

"Any?" the other replied, scarcely containing a chuckle; "only all of them, sir."

Mr. Loch asked to have the latest applications, and the other obsequiously brought the tickets and led the secretary to a private room. At first he found little to shed light upon Father Whitechapel's whereabouts; but then, coming upon a set of case notes that gave him the signpost he was seeking, Mr. Loch quickly left the district office, making his way on foot to a nearby lodging house on Spectacle Alley.

It was by this time about nine in the morning, and the first fog of the season. A great chocolate-coloured pall lowered over heaven, but the wind was continually charging and routing these embattled vapours, so that as he trod from street to street, Mr. Loch beheld a marvellous number of degrees and hues of twilight. Here it would be dark, and there would be a glow of a rich, lurid brown, like the light of some strange conflagration; and here, for a moment, the fog would be quite broken up, and a haggard shaft of daylight would glance in between the swirling wreaths.

Mr. Loch found the front door to the building unlocked; and letting himself in and finding the targeted flat, he knocked sharply at the narrow door, once and then again and yet again, until he heard a rustling within; then a woman's voice called through gruffly: "Rent's not owed till tomorrow."

"It is not about that," Mr. Loch answered. "I am from the Charity Organisation Society, here in regard to your application for relief." To expedite the matter, he slid his card under her door and waited a few minutes, until the door swung open sharply and he was grudgingly admitted into the room. There was only one rickety chair, which Mr. Loch sat down upon, while the small woman arranged herself on the corner of her bed. She was of high cheekbone and large forehead; with hazel eye, fair hair and complexion, though with a noticeable scar on her right cheek, and she appeared, unlike most in the district, to be well-nourished.

"You've come to give me some money?" Miss Millett asked abruptly.

"Not quite," he replied. "I am here to learn more about you and your situation, so we can determine how best to assist you."

"I've already answered the other lady's questions," the woman bristled; "either help me or not, and if not, then you can be going."

"Take heed, miss," Mr. Loch said, narrowing his steely eyes. "I am simply trying to clarify a point of information that will speed this process."

At this she scowled, but sat silently, waiting. "Well, what is it?"

"I see that you've listed as a character reference someone named Father Whitechapel," Mr. Loch began. "I would like to speak to him regarding your case. Do you have an address for him?"

Yet if uncouth, the young woman was shrewd, and now looked at Mr. Loch suspiciously. "I don't know that. And anyway, I'm not so sure he would want to talk to you."

"If he truly wants to help you, I think he would indeed speak to me," Mr. Loch answered. But then, realising the situation, he withdrew from his purse a pound-note. "A token of my appreciation, if you are inclined to cooperate." Even as Mr. Loch made this offer, he winced inwardly, but the strategy took quick effect: her eyes alighted at the money, which she promptly snatched from his hand and held tight in her own.

"I don't know it exact," Miss Millett said, but she was able to recall the name of the road on which Father Whitechapel kept his room. "Good God!" thought Mr. Loch, "can he actually keep residence on such a damnable street?"

"Perhaps you might walk with me and show me the building?" was what the secretary said aloud. "There is another pound in it."

"All right, then," Miss Millett said, donning a soft felt hat with a feather. "But I don't expect him there now. He is never around during the daytime."

The two of them left the tenement, heading eastward as the fog lifted a little and showed a welter of blackguardly surroundings: dingy streets, gin palaces, a low French eating-house, a shop for the retail of penny numbers and twopenny salads, many ragged children huddled in the doorways, and many women of different nationalities passing out, key in hand, to have a morning glass. This was a common enough scene, but one ridden with such unending squalor and continued dirt that Mr. Loch, observing the failing ward, was conscious of some futility in trying to assist its submerged residents, who evidently cared nothing for order and hygiene.

They finally arrived at a doorway in a by-street that bore in every feature the marks of prolonged and dismal negligence. The door, equipped with neither bell nor knocker, seemed welcoming of every sordid drifter. Tramps slouched into the recess and struck matches on the panels; children kept shop upon the steps; the schoolboy had tried his knife on the mouldings; and for generations, no one had appeared to drive away these random visitors or to repair their ravages.

A wizened and silvery-haired old woman stood at the entranceway, eyeing the pair defiantly. She had a homely face, battered by poverty, and manners to match. "You won't be using my rooms for that, Lizzie," she barked out, "so keep along."

Mortified to the quick, his Adam's-apple leaping up his neck, Mr. Loch hastily informed the woman that she was far mistaken in her assumption. "We are looking for Father Whitechapel," he said. "I believe this is where he calls home?"

Yes, the surly woman said, this was where Father White-chapel often slept, but he was not at home; he had been in that night very late, but had gone away again very quickly; there was nothing strange in that; his habits were very irregular, and he was often absent; although he paid the rent without fail and often gave her extra money—"for kindness," she said, with a choke of emotion.

"Very well, then," said the secretary; "but at least you will show me which room is his?"

Looking Mr. Loch up and down, noting his fine clothing and smooth hands, the crone huffed, declared that that was impossible, and then slammed the door in his face.

"You have what you wanted," Miss Millett snapped, thrusting forward her hand, before Mr. Loch had even a chance to react to the landlady's snub. "I'll have my pound now."

He tendered the note with a sigh; and then, clipped and cordial: "We will inform you about your application. In the meantime, be prudent, and—"

But the secretary had not finished his sentence, nor bid the woman goodbye, when she unceremoniously turned away from him and stalked off back toward her home, leaving Mr. Loch to totter away, disturbed at these encounters and even more so, his own laxity of conduct, which may assail even the most honest, in times of desperation.

Search for Father Whitechapel

Dear Sir,—With regard to that phantom charity, the soulless, heartless Charity Organisation Society: this organisation claims it is not merely a dispensary of charitable relief, and this excuse serves very well when it denies relief to persons who on all right principle ought to have it. That *something* is given away is, no doubt, the bait by which the thousands a year are drawn into the office at Buckingham Street. It is a pity that people do not trouble themselves a little more about proportion, and ask themselves how much of the money that flows there is expended on any charitable purpose whatever, and how much is spent upon a nice snuggery of secretaries and clerks, with easy work and good pay, and an army of scouts, spies, and private informers, whose interest and aim it is to run down characters and make up a report in reference to merit and demerit, according to the arbitrary standard of the Society.

It is strange that this society which in every way shrinks from investigation itself should be so ready to play the part of amateur detectives and apply the torture of unnecessary investigation to others. They call in an applicant, who merely wants to feed a hungry family, and what then? Old sores are rubbed up against him, old wounds laid bare until they bleed afresh, and the agonised victim is glad to make his escape from the torture chamber which he was induced to enter by the false hope of relief. Anything more un-English in spirit and sentiment than this human vivisection is impossible to imagine.

Those paid philanthropists and subsidised saints of Buckingham Street might learn something from Father Whitechapel, a true saint, who loves and helps the poor, rather than investigating them. Will *The Times* publish a means by which citizens may send contributions to his noble endeavour? I know many men and women who would take the opportunity gratefully.

Yours faithfully, A. K. ARNOLD
The Christian Men's Union, London.

FROM THAT TIME FORWARD, Mr. Loch began to haunt that lodging house in Whitechapel, carrying a heavy cane so that he might be found in some posture of self-defence; and standing his post late at night under the face of the fogged city moon or by the first glints of sunrise before office hours. The dismal quarter of Whitechapel as seen under these changing glimpses, with its muddy ways, slatternly passengers, and its lamps, which had never been extinguished or had been kindled afresh to combat this mournful re-invasion of darkness, seemed, in the secretary's eyes, like a district of some city in a nightmare. Yet he was determined on his goal and pressed on resolutely, waiting for that lucky strike, and at last his patience was rewarded.

It was a fine, dry night, frost in the air, and in spite of the low growl of London from all round, very quiet. Small sounds carried far; domestic sounds out of the houses were clearly audible on either side of the roadway; and the sound of any pedestrian's gait preceded him by a long time. Mr. Loch had been some minutes at his post, when the stillness was broken by an odd, light footstep drawing near. In the course of his nightly patrols he had long grown accustomed to the quaint effect with which the footfalls of a single person, while he is still a great way off, suddenly spring out distinct from the vast hum and clatter of the city. Yet his attention had never before been so sharply and decisively piqued, and it was with a strong prevision of success that he withdrew into the entry of the court.

The steps drew swiftly nearer, and swelled out suddenly louder as they turned the end of the street. Looking forth from the entry, Mr. Loch could soon see the manner of the man he had been stalking for so long. He was, as described, very tall and very slim, and remarkably graceful in his movements, so that the secretary feared he would miss him entirely; but as his quarry passed by and made to slip through the blistered and distained doorway, Loch lunged out and touched him on the shoulder. "Father Whitechapel, I think?"

The figure shrank back with a sharp intake of breath and halted in his movements, though he answered genially enough: "Yes, brother. What can I do for you?"

"I am Mr. Loch, of the Charity Organisation Society," returned the secretary, feeling the man's warm glow. "I come in regard to Miss Rose Millett. She has applied for aid, and listed you as a reference."

"The poor child," Father Whitechapel answered, appearing to reflect on this for a moment; "do help her. She has many troubles, but her heart is good."

"Well," said the secretary, "we will take that into consideration."

"You have my gratitude, brother," Father Whitechapel
smiled, making to enter the building, but Mr. Loch detained
him: "By the bye, I am glad to have finally met you, since we
have a common friend, in Geoffrey Bodkin."

A close observer might have gathered that the comment
was disconcerting; but Father Whitechapel did not lose his
poise. He merely bowed his head, saying, "Yes, brother, he has
been most kind to me. On your side, though, may I ask how
you come to know that? Has Mr. Bodkin mentioned it to
you?"

"He has not," was the terse reply; "but I am well connected
in this city." To this Father Whitechapel made no response;
and Loch continued with his planned statement. "I say, too,
that I have heard of your charity to one and all. Perhaps you
mean well, but it is most unwise. A penny given, you know, is
a child ruined."

The other sighed aloud with unnerving mournfulness. "Ay,
brother, judge not, that ye be not judged," he murmured, and
the next moment, with extraordinary swiftness, disappeared
into the house.

The secretary stood awhile, much bewildered, when Father
Whitechapel had left him. Then he began slowly to mount
the street, pausing every step or two and shaking his head.
The problem he was thus debating as he walked was of a class
that is rarely solved. This pale, lean figure gave an impression
of frailty without any nameable deficiency; he had a pleasing
smile; he had borne himself to the secretary with a very pretty
manner of politeness and not a whit of subterfuge or dissem-
bling; he spoke with a feminine, whispering and somewhat
fading voice. All these were points for a general decency in his

constitution; but all of these together did not excuse his fool-hardy aid, or his dangerous association with Bodkin, with which Mr. Loch was far from pleased; for how damaging to the Society if it came to light that one of its high officers was slyly sustaining just the sort of haphazard relief so reviled by the organisation.

"Poor Bodkin," the secretary thought, "my mind misgives me he is in deep waters! He was naïve when he was young; a long while ago to be sure; but early marks run deep. Ay, it must be that; or yet it may just as well be the guilt of some business sins now condoning this foolish charity.

"But there must be something else," Loch pondered further; "something more, if I could find a name for it. God bless me, the man seems hardly human! Something ethereal, a mere spirit, and yet with something undeniably spellbinding about him. Some wandering mystic? Or yet out to swindle a trusting soul? The last, I fear; for, O my poor Bodkin, if ever I met a beguiling face, it is that of your new associate."

But now Mr. Loch conceived a spark of hope. "This Father Whitechapel, if he were studied," thought he, "must have secrets of his own, some Jack-in-the-Box of fault. He cannot be so pure as it seems. Yes, he must be proselytising; or, likely enough, endeavouring to stir the labourers into trouble-making. It turns me cold to think of this creature threatening the good name of Geoffrey; poor Geoffrey, what a duping! Ay, things cannot continue as they are. I must put my shoulder to the wheel, and make clear to him the danger of his new friendship. If Bodkin will but listen," he added; "if Bodkin will only listen."

The Banker

BUSINESS APPOINTMENTS.
Geoffrey Bodkin, Esq., of St. James, has been admitted a partner in firm of Coutts & Co., bankers, of 59, Strand, London, W.C. He joined the esteemed bank as a clerk and has had no small share in the successful management of the institution over the last two decades. His clients include merchants and nobility, and to his financial skill many great men have been indebted for many valuable suggestions. *The Times.* December 3, 1888.

A FEW EVENINGS LATER, MR. LOCH and his wife gave one of their pleasant dinners to some five or six council members, all intelligent, reputable men and all judges of good character; and the secretary so contrived to detain Mr. Bodkin after the others had departed, in the guise of discussing a few particulars of Society finances. This was no new arrangement, but a thing that had befallen many times and was much to Bodkin's pleasure. If Loch was not London's most well-liked, he was still a well-placed man, with history and influence in high circles. Gentlemen loved to bask in the company of the dry secretary after the strain of more wayward activities, even resisting the calls of business that they might ease their consciences in the man's unassailable moral stature, or avail themselves of Mr. Loch's counsel in regard to their own charitable conduct. To this rule, Mr. Bodkin was no exception, and as he now sat on the opposite side of the secretary, practising for probity, you could see by his expression that he held for Mr. Loch an approved respect.

"I have been wanting to speak to you on something, Bodkin," began the secretary, after a little rambling talk. "You know that addendum of yours?"

Mr. Bodkin temporized for a bit, his thick frame sitting like a boulder in the room. "My poor Loch," said he, "you are unfortunate in such a treasurer. It was merely a suggestion for financial restructuring, to help a struggling district and perhaps dispel some criticisms of the Society. I had not intended on such a violent reaction, especially from a council of so-called charitable men. Why, I might as well have been talking with that heartless miser, Meade, on what he calls the economic heresy of charity."

"That aside," returned Loch, "your concerns are not wholly unjustified, and in that line, perhaps you would be willing to contribute yourself to our district aid fund. A thousand pounds, say, would go quite a ways."

The face of Mr. Bodkin tensed; his teeth gnashed together; there came a guardedness about his eyes. "I cannot do that at this time," he groused. "My capital is heavily invested."

"I see," Mr. Loch answered, with a note of something like triumph in his voice. "But in that case, perhaps I should ask your new friend, Father Whitechapel? He seems quite liberal with your money."

Mr. Bodkin looked for a moment as if a pistol shot had rang out in the room; but he carried it off coolly. "So you found that out, did you? Well, it is a shame that certain people in this city have long tongues. I am surprised, though, Charles, that you should perpetuate such gossip."

"Steady, sir," Loch continued; "I came into that quite unexpectedly, and I assure you that no one else knows. But yes, I have been learning something of Father Whitechapel. A dangerous fellow, Bodkin, quite out of line with Society principles."

"I understand your opposition," returned the treasurer. "And I know you spoke to him; he told me so. Still, I would prefer to drop the subject. I am oddly situated, Loch; my position is a very strange one. It is one of those affairs that cannot be described."

"Geoffrey," said Mr. Loch, "you know me: I am a man to be trusted. Make a clean breast of this, and I shall make it my business to see you are no loser."

"My good sir," spoke Bodkin, with a certain incoherency of manner; "that is kind of you, and I thank you, but there is one point I should like you to understand. I have really a great respect for this man. I know his work must seem abominable to you. But I do sincerely have a certain affection for that Good Samaritan; and if I seem to be divided in my attentions, I wish you to bear with me. I think you would have greater sympathy, for me at least, if you knew all."

"You know I shall never approve of such reckless charity," said the secretary.

"I do not ask for that. I only ask for patience, at least for a short while, for my sake. Besides, the story is at an end, anyway," mumbled the banker. "The connexion was a fleeting one, and I shall bid goodbye to Father Whitechapel. I give you my hand upon that."

Loch reflected a little, looking in the fire. "I do not doubt your word," he said at last, "but I can't pretend to think well of this friendship of yours."

"That I know," answered Mr. Bodkin, "but truly, Charles, I am loyal to our Society, and I ask you not to deprive me of serving it. In fact"—the banker paused in quick calculation—"I suppose it only fair that I make the donation you mentioned. A thousand pounds, it was?"

The secretary looked over with a disapproving expression. "My dear sir, I did not intend to put you in such a position. I am concerned about your reputation, as I must be, given your standing in the Society; but what you do with your money remains your own business."

"Quite so," Bodkin replied firmly. "And as such, please accept this gift in good faith, and allow me to add one word: this is a private matter, Charles, and I beg of you to let it sleep."

Loch heaved an uneasy sigh. "Well," said he, getting to his feet, "so be it, then."

MURDER AT POPLAR.

WOMAN FOUND STRANGLED.
IS IT THE RIPPER?

Yesterday Mr. Wynne E. Baxter, Coroner, opened an inquiry as to the death of an unknown woman, whose body was found lying in a yard attached to the premises of Mr. Clarke, builder, of High-street, Poplar, early on Thursday morning.

Police-sergeant Robert Golding, 26 K, deposed that he was patrolling High-street, Poplar, on Thursday morning about 4 15. While passing Mr. Clarke's yard he saw something lying under the wall, and going close found it to be the body of woman. She was lying on her left side, her left arm underneath her. The right leg was at full length, and her left leg slightly drawn up. The body was quite warm. Her clothes were not disarranged, nor could he detect any mutilation of the body. She was lying under the wall, with her head away from the street. The witness left the constable in charge of the body while he went for the divisional surgeon.

Dr. Harris, the assistant, returned with him and examined the body before it was moved. He at once pronounced life to be extinct. The witness then sent for the ambulance, and the body was taken to the mortuary. He searched it and made an examination of the clothing. Round the neck the deceased was wearing a blue-spotted handkerchief, tied loosely. There was no string round the neck. In the pocket of the dress he found 1s. in silver and 3½d. in bronze, together with a few papers. The woman was about 5ft. 2in. high, had light hair, hazel eyes, and hair frizzed close to the head. She was wearing a black alpaca dress, brown stuff skirt, and red flannel petticoat. She also had on a dark tweed jacket, double-breasted, a lilac print apron, blue and red striped stockings, and side-spring boots. A felt hat with a feather was found near the spot. The witness said he believed he had seen the woman before, and that she was of loose character. The yard in which the body of this woman was found is a dark and neglected byway.

Mr. Matthew Brownfield, of East India-road, Poplar, deposed that he was divisional surgeon of police. Yesterday morning the witness saw the body in the mortuary and subsequently made a post-mortem examination. He found the body to be that of a woman about 30 years of age and well nourished. He noticed marks of mud on the front of the left leg. The eyes were normal and the tongue did not protrude. There were slight marks of blood having escaped from the nostrils, and the right side of the nose showed a large bruise, while on the left cheek was an old scar. The mark on the nose might have been caused by any slight violence. On the neck there were deep marks extending from the right side of the spine round the throat to the lobe of the left ear. He had, by experiment, found that his thumb and fingers could cause such abrasions.

From his examination he was of opinion that the cause of death was suffocation by strangulation. The strangulation could not possibly have been done by the woman herself, but must have been caused by a person facing and slightly to the left of her.

The mystery surrounding the murder can only be compared to that which attended the recent series of crimes in the same district. At a late hour last night the police had no one in custody in connexion with the crime.

The Clarke's Yard Murder Case

LATE THAT PAST SUMMER, as though stepped out from a penny dreadful, there arose in Whitechapel a shadowy villain dubbed the Ripper, hunting and slaying with gruesome method, one prostitute after another, five in all throughout the last quarter of the year; each dispatched in utter darkness and left incredibly mangled, with very few clues that might lead to the monster's capture. The crimes were a black mark on London, a source of much embarrassment to the hapless lawmen; and all the city was gripped by the sensationalised accounts of the Ripper.

Mr. Loch, as well, took keen notice of the slaughters, though for a singular and idiosyncratic reason. The concentration of these murders to Whitechapel; the seeming invisibility of the fugitive; his familiarity with the area's lowest women; the convenient cover of doling out relief,—all of this inflamed Loch's curiosity, and he could not help but to speculate on a linkage, or rather overlap, between the Ripper and Bodkin's mysterious new associate.

A few days before Christmas, the secretary's suspicions finally came to a head. London was again startled by the grisly murder of another known prostitute, achieved by brutal strangulation and the body recovered in Clarke's Yard, a grim rookery off of Poplar High Street. As always, details were sparse; yet deposing the courtyard's inhabitants finally yielded what was thus far the strongest lead on this baffling case. It seemed that an unemployed dockworker had come out of a public-house about eleven at night and stumbled over to Clarke's Yard, but lacking the two pence needed for a bed, had settled for sleeping in one of the doorways. Never (he said, when narrating the experience), never had he felt so outraged at the injustices of life or thought more bitterly of the upper classes. And as he curled upon the splintery wood, he dozed for some time, awakening in the middle of the night to the sound of voices. Just then he became aware of a beautiful gentleman with whitish hair tending to a "woman o' the night," as the onlooker called her. Even in his stupor, he recognised a certain Father Whitechapel, who often visited the yard and for whom he had conceived a great liking.

The moon shone on Father Whitechapel's face as he spoke to the young woman, and the labourer was pleased to watch it, for the pale man seemed to breathe such an innocent and old-world kindness of disposition, yet with something high too, as of a well-founded self-content. Presently the labourer nodded off, yet was awakened later by a cry; and as he looked on drowsily, the figure suddenly became a whirlwind of ape-like fury, felling the woman to the earth with a heavy blow, and audibly throttling her as her body jumped upon the roadway. So horrifying was this scene that the man took it for a hallucination or a nightmare, and dropped back into his doze, until the commotion of the crime scene brought him to himself early next morning.

At first the woman could not be identified satisfactorily, for everyone seemed to put forth a different name for her; but then from the tattered papers found in her purse, Mr. Loch's card came out. Accordingly, the latter was requested to come to the police station, and at the beckon he dressed quickly, hurrying through breakfast, and drove to the station, where he met with one Police-sergeant Golding. As soon as he came into the room wither the body had been carried, he nodded and shot out a solemn lip.

"Yes," said he, looking down at the corpse, "I recognise her. Her name, to the best of my knowledge, is Rose Millett."

"Ah! Finally. And we may have gotten a bit of luck this time," the officer said, animated with ambition; and he briefly narrated what the vagrant had related.

The secretary listened to the account with a grave countenance; though at the mention of Father Whitechapel, his eyes lighted up. "Is this man a person of tall stature, and very thin?"

"Particularly tall and particularly pale-faced, is what the man called him," said the officer. "Perhaps you know something of this Father Whitechapel?"

Mr. Loch reflected; and then, raising his head: "If you will come with me in my cab, I think I can take you to his house."

Once again the secretary travelled through that sordid warren of the East End, back to the lodging house that the late Miss Millett had pointed out to him; and once again the old shrew barred the doorway, declaring that she would allow no one into her rooms, especially not those who came looking for Father Whitechapel, as so many did, for she was under strict orders to maintain his privacy.

"I had better tell you who this person is," Loch snapped back. "This is Sergeant Golding of the Criminal Investigation Division."

A flash of patent shock appeared upon the woman's face. "No!" cried she, "he is not in trouble? It can't be. A fallen angel, that is, by my eye."

"My good woman," the officer said, "we wish to avoid a scene. Now just let me and this gentleman have a look about us."

The three of them trod upstairs, stepping carefully for lack of banisters, all having been destroyed for kindling. In the whole extent of the house, which was full to bursting with wailing children, bickering mothers and raging men, Father Whitechapel had only used one tiny room, and this must have been the very worst of the worst. The room's sole furnishing consisted of a bed of straw and rags; there was a stove, but this appeared unusable; otherwise the quarters were utterly barren. Grime coated every surface; the floorboards were visibly rotted; vermin scurried about freely; nowhere was any sort of washing facility; and there was throughout the building a stench so overpowering that Loch could just keep from retching. This—*this*, was the home of Geoffrey Bodkin's favourite, he reflected sadly, thinking of his friend's high place at the bank and his illustrious clients.

The search of the room took only a few moments, but feeling through the rags upon which this beloved character slept, the officer extracted a black Gladstone bag, empty, which Loch supposed was the very same satchel that Snell had seen, as well as a small note-book enrobed with black leather, quite as his Society investigator had mentioned. With these in hand, the sergeant and the secretary hurried from the building's fetid fumes and jarring noises, and once returned to the station, the two men began perusing the contents of the book, which contained page upon page of names and addresses, although in most cases the paper was so filthy and the ink so smudged that little was legible. Yet the sergeant's eyes stopped upon a certain grouping of pages; he peered closer and read aloud a series of women's names, which sounded vaguely familiar to the secretary.

"Do you know what those are?" Golding remarked. "All of the Ripper victims to this point, and their usual haunts writ beside."

"Is that so?" Mr. Loch returned, his eyes narrowing at this revelation.

"At minimum, sir," the officer said, "I have enough to make an arrest. It may turn out to be nothing, but it may not. And now we only have to get out the handbills, and keep an eye on the tenement house."

This last, however, was not so easy of accomplishment; while Father Whitechapel had numbered many familiars, all of whom expressed love and gratitude for the man, his family could nowhere be traced; he had never been photographed; and those who described him differed widely, as common observers will. Only on one point were they agreed—inexplicably enough, given this new turn of events—and that was the haunting sense of unearthly goodness with which the fugitive impressed upon his beholders.

Incident of the Account Book

FIVE HUNDRED POUNDS REWARD.
THE POPLAR MURDER. Whereas ROSE
MILLETT, aged 29, was found strangled, at
Clarke's-yard, Poplar High Street, on December
22nd. The murder is supposed to have been committed by a man who goes by the alias of "Father
Whitechapel," of the following description, who was
seen in the company with the deceased on the night
in question and is strongly suspected of having been
concerned in the said murder: tall, slim build, complexion fair, clean-shaven, dressed very plainly in
black or brown, often seen with black satchel and
black note-book in hand. The wanted man is also
thought to have been involved in the recent outrages
in the East End. FIVE HUNDRED POUNDS
REWARD will be paid by Her Majesty's Govern-
ment to any person who shall give such information
and evidence as shall lead to the discovery of the
murderer; and the Secretary of State for the House
Department will advise the grant of Her Majesty's
most gracious pardon to any accomplice not being
the person who actually committed the murder, who
shall give such evidence as shall lead to a like result.
Information to the Director of Criminal Investiga-

tion, Great Scotland-yard, London, England, or at any Metropolitan Police-station. *East London Advertiser*. January 4, 1889.

NOT LONG AFTER HE LEFT the police station, Mr. Loch found his way to Mr. Bodkin's door, where he was admitted by Spencer and carried down by the kitchen offices and across a yard to the building which was indifferently known as the laboratory. The banker had bought the house from the estate of a celebrated physician, and for some reason unknown to Loch, had not changed the destination of the block back from a laboratory into a garden. It was the first time that the secretary had been received in that part of his friend's quarters; now he eyed the dingy, windowless structure with curiosity, and as he crossed the theatre, gazed round with a distasteful sense of strangeness at the tables laden with chemical apparatus, the floor strewn with crates and littered with packing straw, and the light falling dimly through the foggy cupola.

At the further end, a flight of stairs mounted to a door covered with red baize, and through this Mr. Loch was at last received into the cabinet. It was a large room looking out upon the court by three dusty windows barred with iron; outfitted with glass presses and furnished with, among other things, a cheval-glass and a business table. A fire burned in the grate and a lamp was set lighted on the chimney shelf, for even in the house the fog began to lie thickly; and there, close up to the warmth, sat Mr. Bodkin, looking very low and very disturbed. The banker did not rise to meet his visitor, but held out a cold hand and bade him welcome in a changed voice.

"And now," said Mr. Loch, as soon as Spencer had left them, "you have heard the news?"

Bodkin shuddered. "They were crying it in the square," he answered. "I heard them in my dining room."

"One word," said the secretary. "You have not been mad enough to hide this fellow?"

"Loch, I swear to God," cried the banker, "I swear to God, he is not behind these atrocities. I bind my honour on that. The police are mistaken; in the pitch of the moment they have pointed at the wrong man."

"I tell you, Bodkin," said Loch, gravely: "it does not look good. London is eager for a culprit, and the case against your man is somewhat convincing. The detectives are set upon arresting him."

"Then it is all at an end," Mr. Bodkin muttered darkly. "But you must believe me," he continued, in a pained, wheezing voice; "you do not know him as I do; he is perfectly harmless."

The secretary listened gloomily; he did not like his friend's feverish manner. "You seem pretty sure of him," said he; "and for your sake, I hope you are right. If it came to a trial, your name might appear."

"I am quite sure of him," replied Bodkin. "I have grounds for certainty that I cannot share with any one, but I ask you to trust me on this matter."

Loch gazed grimly into the fire. "I wonder," he finally spoke, "if it would be best for you to suspend your duties with the Society, at least until all of this passes."

The banker seemed seized with a qualm of faintness, though he recovered quickly and sat up straight in his chair. "I promise you that is not necessary. I am quite done with all of this, and with him. Mark my words, he will never more be heard of. Besides, it might look the worse if I leave so suddenly. Let things remain as they are, and I pledge that all of this will be put to rights." Mr. Bodkin reached to a table for a packet of papers. "In fact, here is the new treasury report. You will find it reflects the contribution previously discussed, but credited to the discretionary fund, for you to employ as you see fit."

Loch ruminated awhile, surprised by his friend's defensiveness, and yet relieved by it, for it seemed a return of Bodkin's typical self-interest. "But one word more," said he, accepting the packet; "it was Father Whitechapel who dictated that addendum of yours?"

Bodkin squirmed under a pang of guilt, but shut his mouth tight and nodded.

"I knew it," said Loch. "And now he turns out to be wanted for murder. Well, at any rate, he has certainly drawn attention to the Whitechapel district, if that was his aim. Let us only pray your own reputation escapes unsullied."

"What is far more to the point," returned the other solemnly; "let us pray for an end to London's horrors. O God, Loch, what horrors this city bears!" And he covered his face for a moment with his hands.

On his way out, the secretary stopped and had a word with Spencer. "Forgive me," said he, "but has anyone besides myself come to the house today? Perhaps through the side door?"

Spencer said that he had not admitted anyone; though come to think on it, he had heard the distinctive creak and slam of the laboratory door last night. "But that was likely the master, for he often comes and goes that way."

This bit of information sent off Mr. Loch with his fears renewed. Perhaps, he thought gloomily, he had been too lenient with Bodkin, especially if that shadowy figure was still coming and going through the side door. The newsboys, as he went, were crying themselves hoarse along the footways: "Special edition. Shocking twist in Ripper case. Police seek charity man Father Whitechapel." That was the calling card of his friend's associate; and Loch could not help a certain apprehension lest the name of Bodkin should be sucked down in the eddy of the scandal, and take with it the Society.

The next day at the Central Office, as the afternoon drew to a close, Mr. Loch summoned to his office his assistant organising secretary, Mr. Graham. After some passing conversation, Loch brought out the folio given him earlier that day and set it down on the table. "Bodkin's newest treasury report," he said, "quite in your way. Perhaps you wouldn't mind looking it through."

Graham's eyes brightened, being of an accounting background, and he broke the seal at once and began to study the pages. As he did, Loch asked, "What do you think of Mr. Bodkin, Graham?"

"Bodkin?" repeated the assistant, glancing up from the report. "A sharp fellow, clever with money. He's gotten on quite well at Coutts's." Graham, in fact, was not particularly fond of the banker or his appointment as treasurer, but knowing of Loch's long friendship, he spoke with a certain delicacy. "Though I thought that addendum of his to be rather out of sorts."

"I should like to hear your views on that," replied Loch. "What do you suppose makes a man submit such a proposal?"

Graham pondered this for a moment. "That's hard to say, sir. A soft spot in him, perhaps, or fear of public opinion. It's pure foolishness, of course. Whitechapel is a lost cause; everyone knows that. Why, look at the news: the slum's so-called saviour turns out to be a murderer."

"Yes," Loch said; "the public feeling is of much confusion."

"The man, obviously, is mad," returned Graham. "But then again, sir, a few women like that off the streets is hardly much of a loss, is it?" The assistant turned back to reading the report; then, after some minutes of silence, peered closer and appeared to be sedulously examining a certain page. "Hm," he remarked. "It's very interesting."

"What is?" Loch inquired.

"Well, sir," explained the assistant, "there's a rather crafty accounting structure used. I almost missed it myself. The columns appear to match on first glance; but on second look, it seems that a number of administrative expenses have been double-counted."

"Rather peculiar," said Loch.

"It is, as you say, rather peculiar," echoed Graham, with slight sarcastic emphasis. "I don't see why Bodkin would be concealing a shortfall. It doesn't commend itself to reason—unless there is something afoot."

There was a pause, during which Mr. Loch struggled with himself. "You are positive on this, Graham?"

"Yes, sir," was the assistant's reply, showing Loch exactly the discrepancy in the report.

"Most peculiar," Loch reiterated. "But let us not fall prey to exorbitant alarm. It is merely an oversight, I am sure. I will look into it personally. Until then, I wouldn't speak of this, you know."

"No, sir," said Graham, sourly. "I understand."

But no sooner was Mr. Loch alone that night, than he pored over the report again, crushing his temples in his hands. "What!" he thought. "Geoffrey Bodkin an embezzler?" And he chilled to the very bone.

Two Letters

ALLEGED SUICIDE OF A MANUFACTURER.
Much consternation has been caused by the mysterious death of Mr. Wallace Meade, 44, of Mayfair, owner of the Meade Company, a leading clothing manufacturer in London. The deceased was found in his home two nights ago. It appears that on Sunday evening, either by accident or design, he ingested an overdose of morphia. He sunk into stupor, and died on Monday morning. The mystery is compounded by the discovery that just a few days before his death Mr. Meade altered his last will and testament to order his company liquidated upon his death and the proceeds divided equally among the employees. His business partners, friends and family have not the slightest knowledge of anything to justify such action and will endeavour to overturn the will through a court of law, as Mr. Meade is thought to have been of unsound mind when amending it. The case has been referred to Mr. Wynne E. Baxter, Coroner. *Daily News.* February 20, 1889.

TIME RAN ON; THE REWARD MOUNTED into thousands of pounds, for the murders were resented as a public terror; but Father Whitechapel had disappeared out of the ken of the police as though he had never existed. Much of his past was unearthed, but ironically, it read like a hagiography: tales came out of the man's selfless and devoted charity; of his spotless life and the Christ-like passion that surrounded his career; but of his present whereabouts, not a whisper. From the time he had fled Clarke's Yard on the night of the murder, he was simply blotted out. The lodging house remained on constant watch for some time, but eventually this was given up, for never did Father Whitechapel show himself anywhere near the building.

There had been a fright among the Society council, for the dead prostitute had applied several times to the Society for a mangle, to earn a more honest living, but had been rejected each time, with the explanation that there were already too many mangles in the neighbourhood and little chance of her profiting from the investment. And while Mr. Loch stood by the decision, his critics nonetheless descended like harpies, pointing to the Society and its "gospel of the buttoned pocket" (so went the popular slur) as having a hand in the dreadful murder. Yet the embattled secretary soldiered on, ever deflecting attention to Father Whitechapel, who was, after all, still the chief suspect in the Ripper case. And Loch's face was nearly lighted by a smile when some of the East Enders who had eulogised Father Whitechapel began, with herd-like mentality, to hunt the latter relentlessly, eager for the fat bounty.

Gradually the tempest subsided, and Mr. Loch began to recover from the hotness of his alarm. The deaths of the streetwalkers were, to his way of thinking, more than paid for by the disappearance of Father Whitechapel, and now that that perverting influence had been withdrawn, a new life began for Mr. Bodkin. He came out of his seclusion, renewed relations with his friends on the council, became once more their familiar guest and entertainer; and whilst he had always been known for his work at Coutts's, he was now no less diligent for the Society. He was busy, he was much out and about, he did well for himself, and for more than two months, the banker was at peace with prosperity. Loch himself was so pleased by Bodkin's recovery from that bout of moral insanity that he closed his eyes to the matter of the account-book, granting his friend a rare pardon.

On the 8th of January Loch dined at Meade's with a small party; Bodkin had been there and seemed his usual self; yet the Society council meeting on the Monday following was without Bodkin's attendance or prior notice thereof. Mr. Loch relayed that commitments at the bank were the cause of the treasurer's absence, but he frowned inwardly, dreading to think what it perhaps signified. Already there had been murmurs among the council regarding Bodkin's somewhat erratic behaviour of late: one moment submitting that fault-finding addendum; another, making a handsome donation to the organisation; and thus there was lingering doubt, certainly in the suspicious Graham, as to the real cause of the treasurer's absenteeism. In fact, in the course of conversation after the meeting adjourned, Mr. Loch overheard Mr. Graham expressing his concern to Mr. Thornton. "It seems, unfortunately, that Bodkin is drifting apart from our mission," Graham murmured, "and besides that, I noticed a few oddities in the Society's account-book."

"Oddities?" repeated Thornton. "What do you mean there?"

At this, Mr. Loch interceded in the discussion and cleared his throat for attention. "Pardon me, gentlemen, but the point in question was that Mr. Bodkin employed a complicated accountancy structure, confusing to the untrained eye. Keep in mind that our treasurer's business is balance-sheets, so let us defer to, and be grateful for, his expertise."

Shortly after, Mr. Loch took his assistant aside and asked, with something of a huff, what he meant by spreading rumours about Mr. Bodkin.

"Forgive me, sir," Graham replied defiantly, "but there is something wrong. I don't like it."

"Nor do I," the secretary answered. "However, I see no call for anyone else to be involved until we know the truth of the matter."

With that, Loch concluded his farewells and then travelled, with some urgency, to Bodkin's house. But when he arrived and was greeted at the front door by Spencer, the latter informed Mr. Loch that the master was seeing no one, and when Loch pushed for some amount of information, the butler had, indeed, no very pleasant news to communicate. His master, it appeared, now more than ever confined himself to the cabinet over the laboratory, where he would sometimes even sleep; he was out of spirits; he stayed home on many business days; it seemed as if something very troubling was on his mind.

Mr. Loch was amazed; the dangerous sway of Father Whitechapel seemed to have gone away; Bodkin had returned to his old tasks and amities; a week ago, the banker had smiled with every promise of a cheerful and an honoured age—and now in a moment, friendship, duty, and the whole tenor of his life were wrecked. As soon as he got home, Loch sat down and wrote to Bodkin, complaining of his exclusion from the house as well as his neglect of Society business; and the next morning brought him a long answer, often very pathetically worded, and darkly mysterious in drift.

No longer, wrote Bodkin, could he serve the Society; his post was to be considered resigned. "I mean from henceforth to lead a life of extreme seclusion," he wrote. "You must not be surprised, nor must you doubt my friendship, if my door is often shut even to you. You must suffer me to go my own sad way. I could not think that this earth contained reversals so unmanning; and you can do but one thing, Charles, to lighten this destiny: that is to open your hand to those in need, and beyond that, to respect my silence."

Mr. Loch was further astonished; so great and unprepared a change pointed to madness; but in view of the banker's manner and words, there must lie for it some deeper ground; and the secretary said nothing to the council of Bodkin's resignation, hoping that the banker might yet get it to his mind to reverse his decision. Loyalty to an old friend ran strong in Mr. Loch; yet in his heart, he felt that Bodkin had gone wrong, wrong in mind, and the secretary feared to ally himself too closely with that impenetrable hermit, whose life now teetered on the verge of disaster.

Later that evening, when Mr. Loch and his wife were reading together, she paused to ask how Mr. Bodkin was doing these days, and if he were still a bachelor.

"Bodkin?" he said sharply. "Why do you ask that? What have you heard?"

"Why, nothing," Mrs. Loch replied, with the air of one very much surprised and a trifle hurt. "Miss Chivers mentioned him today, and wondered if I might introduce them."

Loch pondered this, though it seemed nothing new: around such a wealthy and influential bachelor as Bodkin, there had long buzzed a cloud of matrimonial suitors. "I do not think I shall be able to ask him," he answered. "He will not see me of late."

"Oh?" his wife asked. "What has happened?"

There was no person from whom he kept fewer secrets than his wife, but now Mr. Loch held up a trembling hand. "Sophie, my dear, speak not of Mr. Bodkin," he pleaded. "I am quite troubled with that person; and I beg that you spare me any allusion to one who seems quite willing to destroy himself, and with it, all that I have worked for."

"Charles," his wife said, in an awed tone, "those are hard words for an old friend; you may not outlive them. Can't anything be done?"

"I cannot say," returned he, in a loud, unsteady voice. "And in the meantime, my dear, if you can sit and talk with me of other things, for God's sake, do so; but if you cannot keep clear of this accursed topic, then let us say good-night, for I cannot bear it."

The mood in Loch's household was indeed ominous over the next few days; and this only worsened when the unsettling death of Mr. Meade was announced. Two days later was the funeral, at which Mr. Loch was sadly affected and which Bodkin did not attend; and oddly enough, when the secretary arrived home, there was waiting for him an envelope addressed by the hand and sealed with the seal of his dead friend, just a few days ago, now seeming as though from beyond the grave.

Mr. Loch, who had already been brooding worriedly that Meade's suicide and the strange clause of his will were somehow connected to the same evil that seemed to have overwhelmed Bodkin, now quailed at the letter and dreaded to behold the contents. But finally, late that night, when the inmates of his house were locked in rigorous slumber, he took to his business room, locked the door behind him, and set before him the envelope. Within it there was another enclosure, sealed in several places, along with a note in Meade's hand and dated at the top:

15th February, 1889.

When this shall fall into your hands, I will be dead. I have had a shock, Charles, and I shall never recover. You will read in the newspaper of my last act of desperate salvation; whether the act can pacify a too just resentment of my career, I have not the penetration to foresee. Judge for yourself. However, if you care to hear of what prompted such morbid action and led me to my final hour, then go forth and read this narrative of your unworthy and unhappy friend,—W.M.

"The man is buried already," Loch thought: "why read something to his disgrace?" But then, condemning his hesitation as fear, and having already pondered too much on Meade's inexplicable death to pause before seeing an end to the enigma, Mr. Loch broke the seal and began to read. Yet the contents only increased his wonder, for this is how the letter ran:

Mr. Meade's Narrative

ON THE 9TH OF FEBRUARY, as you recall, I gave a party at my home; by about midnight, everyone had departed, and it remained only myself and Geoffrey Bodkin, both of us slightly worse for the drink. The idea of taking the "Mile-End tour" in Whitechapel arose, for what licentious purpose I hardly need detail, and off we sped to the task, taking my smallest covered carriage. It was a dark winter night, the light of the moon scarcely visible through the clouds, and it was with some peril that we navigated the alleys of the East End, finally leaving the fly near Assembly Passage, which was quiet and bare of concourse. At that point we parted ways; I settled my business; and as agreed upon, returned to the hansom just as two o'clock was ringing out over London.

But when I climbed into the small carriage, someone other than Bodkin was waiting inside; some rough, I figured, looking for an easy mark, and so I made to grab this person and forcibly eject him. He was perfectly still and made no resistance, but in a hypnotic voice that literally froze me: "Take ease, brother," he said, handing over a folded paper. "I am come from your friend, Geoffrey Bodkin, on business of some moment."

This was much to my surprise: after all, I had seen Bodkin, rode in the cab with him an hour ago, and could imagine nothing that should justify him sending me a letter by way of messenger. Yet no doubt the note was scrawled in Bodkin's large, clunky script, and leaning over to read by glimmer of a street-lamp, this is what I saw:

Wallace,—You are one of my oldest friends, and although we may have differed at times on certain questions, I cannot remember, at least on my side, any break in our affection. Since you and I parted not long ago, I have fallen into an un-nameable danger from which I cannot escape by my own power. My life, my honour, and my reason now depend upon you—if you fail me to-night, I am lost.

I want you to postpone your return to home for the present and ride with my messenger to a certain lodging house. Once there, he will remain in your fly and you, *yourself,* must run an errand for me in the house. The lock on the front door is broken; if a woman should bar your way, a pound or two will be sufficient pass-word. Go to the back room on the uppermost floor; it should be empty; pry up the third floorboard from the southern wall and draw from the space a metal lock-fast box; next carry it back to the fly and give it to my messenger. Then you will have played your part and earned my gratitude completely.

Confident as I am that you will not trifle with this appeal, my heart sinks and my hand trembles at the bare thought of such a possibility. Think of me at this hour, in a strange place, labouring under a blackness of distress that no fancy can exaggerate, and yet well aware that, if you will but punctually serve me, my troubles will cease.

Serve me, my dear Meade, and save,—Your friend, G. B.

A simple request for money might have been somewhat comprehensible, as gentlemen are apt to get into such tangles in the East End—but to sneak into a tenement house, pull up a floor and retrieve a metal box, in the pitch of night? It all sounded quite insane; and if this messenger before me could deliver a letter, what was the impediment of him going to the room himself? Yet I felt bound to do as Bodkin requested. The less I understood of this debacle, the less I was in a position to judge of its importance, and an appeal so worded could not be set aside without grave responsibility.

I looked up at the messenger in wonder. "If I am to travel with you on such an errand," I said, affecting a coolness I was far from truly possessing, "I might at least make your acquaintance."

"Forgive me, brother," he replied in a silky tone. "I am called Father Whitechapel."

I thought I recalled that name as being in the papers for some reason or another, which at the moment evaded me; but I offered my hand, with as fair an imitation of my ordinary manner to any gentleman as the nature of the situation would suffer me to muster. He took my hand into his own, and instantly I was conscious of a certain spread of warmth through my blood. I felt extraordinarily calm, inebriated even (though in a different way than by drink), and the more time I spent in the man's company, the more I felt something abnormal and eerie in the very essence of the creature that now faced me— something seizing, surprising and transfixing, and at the same time seeming to suggest the presence of a nobler soul than I had yet encountered.

"Shall we be off?" he pleaded, rending my heart, for he seemed to be wrestling against the approaches of a fit; and thus we made out for the lodging house, which in the darkness and along the twisted alleys, took some time to reach.

But what that man showed me along that journey, Charles, I cannot bring my mind to set on paper. As for the hell that man unveiled to me, that city of dreadful night, even with tears of penitence and bankrupting charity, I cannot, even in memory, dwell on it without a start of horror. We toured alleys and courtyards so repugnant, populated by men, women and children so pathetic, so degraded by inhuman surroundings and unending moral turpitude, that even now when those sights have faded from my eyes, I ask myself if I believe it, and I cannot answer. I saw what I saw, and my soul sickened at it, yet I could not quell my incredulity.

The lodging house, when finally we arrived, brought only fresh terrors. I did as Bodkin requested, bribing the old woman and then making my way upstairs. Passing one squalid room, I peered inside at a woman hunched over a slanted table, six gaunt children huddled round as her bony fingers buzzed over what I instantly knew to be the unending and profitless sweat-work of piecemeal garment manufacture. Hitherto, I had indulged in the lazy cruelty of neglect, avoiding confrontation of such horrendous reality by virtue of middle-men. Now I could only stare in shock, until she took aware and glared up at me, likely taking me for a rent-collector or sanitation inspector. "Leave us be!" she lashed out, her voice laced with bitter sorrow; then suddenly one of the children hurled a shirt-collar toward me, which struck me in the chest and then dropped to the floor. I bent down to pick up the collar, and sure enough, stitched upon the item, was the very label—"Meade Clothing Company."

I felt faint at this rebuke, so pointed and ugly that it brought out the sweat on me like running; but recalling my task, I scurried to the designated room, where I pried up the rotted boards to indeed find a small metal lock-fast box, sealed in several places, which I brought back to the fly and into the messenger's eagerly waiting hands. "There it is, sir," said I, and seeing the box, he laid his hand upon his heart, sighing and quivering with ecstasy. We drove some more blocks, and reaching a deserted area, the man fled the carriage and glided away.

I do not fault that saintly patron to the poor; I credit him, in fact, with opening my eyes to the unfathomable depths of these human warrens; but now, having seen all, I should be glad to get away. "Dear God, what can I do?" I asked my companion at one point; and he answered: "Take the word of our Lord, brother: go, sell what you have; give to the poor; and you will have treasure in heaven."

So it shall be, though it is already too late for me. My life is shaken to its roots; sleep has left me; the deadliest shame haunts me at all hours of the day and night. I am a damned man; I feel my mercenary life utterly wasted; that I must die and suffer for my arrogance; and yet I shall die ashamed, weeping and howling for the miseries coming upon me, my flesh eaten with fire, for permitting—nay, causing others to live as I saw. Goodbye, then, Charles; heed these words, and pray God you shall not meet me in the hereafter...

WALLACE MEADE

P.S.—I had almost sealed this up when something struck me. It was very dark and my eyes may have failed me, but when that creature departed the cab onto the most deserted street we could find, I noticed that his clothes were far too bulky on him: enormously too broad, the collar sprawling wide upon his shoulders, and yet at the same time far too short for the man, the trousers hanging on his legs with six inches between them and the ground, the waist of the coat above his navel, the sleeves revealing most of the forearms. He had just about vanished from sight when a familiar belt-buckle flashed, and I offer—if you can bring your mind to credit it—that those were the very same clothes Bodkin had been wearing earlier that evening.

Incident at the Bank

I T CHANCED THAT ON A FRIDAY, when Mr. Loch was walking with his assistant Mr. Graham down the bustling Strand, that they came in front of the door to Coutts's bank.

"I don't suppose," Graham inquired, "that you've learned any more from Bodkin on the account-book?"

"I have not yet asked," the secretary replied, blanching for a moment, for he had still not reported Bodkin's eccentric resignation letter. "He has been from home whenever I call."

"That is convenient, isn't it?" the assistant remarked, peevishly. "But in that case, perhaps we step inside and say hello."

Normally the secretary would not presume to impose during banking hours, but given the circumstances, and now after reading Meade's outlandish tale, Loch felt still more uneasy about his friend's well-being. If he could look but once upon Bodkin's face, the secretary thought, he might be able to know if Bodkin was not lost completely, and whether their bond might yet be salvaged. And so the two men entered the stately bricked building, to be greeted by an air of great wealth and comfort. The oak-panelled walls radiated their lustre; cabinets displayed valuable porcelain and china behind sparkling glass, and much to Loch's pleasure, there was everywhere signs of order, diligence and industry; even the clerks' desks and accoutrements were organised with methodical care.

Yet when the secretary and his assistant came to the door of what the former knew to be Bodkin's luxurious office-suite, they found an empty room and an unusually clear desk.

"Pardon me," Mr. Loch said to a passing clerk, "has Geoffrey Bodkin moved to a different room?"

"Mr. Bodkin?" the other returned, with a furrowed brow. "I'm sorry, sir, he is on leave."

"What! On leave!" Loch cried. "For how long?"

"He has not said, sir," the clerk answered. "I believe he is unwell."

Mr. Loch shook his head, struggling to digest this information. The problem of Bodkin now seemed much worsened. It was one thing for him to forfeit his position as Society treasurer, but for that distinguished banker to take leave from his very livelihood, and rather ungracefully, from the look of it—Loch was dumbfounded, helplessly pondering this remarkable turn of events, until he was called to attention by Graham whispering in his ear: "I think it wise, sir, for us to check the books, quite immediately."

"That is just what I was about to venture to propose," grimaced the other, as he turned back to the bank-clerk. "Well," Mr. Loch coughed, "that is news to me. I am sorry to hear that. As long as I am here, however, perhaps you would bring me the account register for the Charity Organisation Society." And he presented his card to the clerk.

The register was given to the secretary, who settled into a chair to review the present state of the Society's finances. Yet even before fully seated, a glance at the tally of available funds made his blood run cold in his veins. Scarcely anything was left; thousands of pounds, it seemed, had been spent without his knowledge, with not even enough left for the wages of the undersecretaries and clerks this month.

Graham could not help but to see the panic in Loch's eyes, and he snatched the register out of the latter's grip to read the tally. "Perhaps now you will believe me that there has been mischief with the accounting," he fumed. "But what to expect? when a wolf guards the hen-house."

Staggered, his face turned a sort of mottled pallor, Loch summoned a bank manager; and fighting to temper his agitation, he inquired if the register was positively correct, and if any unauthorised withdrawals had been made of late.

"One moment, I will check on that," the manager said. "I thank you, sir." But when the latter returned, he confirmed that the balance was accurately stated. Yes, there had been steady withdrawals over the past months, but all by Mr. Bodkin, who was endorsed on the account by Loch himself. "If there is some discrepancy," the manager continued, "you are welcome to speak with our security department."

Mr. Loch meditated on this for a moment, but was again roused by Graham, who drew the secretary aside, where they could speak in private.

"Graham," Loch said solemnly, before the assistant could speak, "this is a sad business, to be sure, but I think it best if I discuss the matter with Mr. Bodkin direct. I may yet be able to recover the money."

"You may do as you please with Bodkin," Mr. Graham hissed. "But what an ass you must think me, that I will go along protecting that scoundrel. No, sir, he will not buy his way out of this one. The council will hear of this, Charles, and vengeance be our name, Bodkin's name will stink from one end of London to the other."

"A stench that will hang on the Society as well," Mr. Loch retorted. "Do you think it possible to slander one without the other?"

The two men exchanged a long glance of disagreement. "That is to be seen, sir," Graham finally returned, "depending on where you come down on the matter." And he took up the account-book and flounced toward the manager's office.

Mr. Loch collected himself, and to avoid further public humiliation, went quickly on his way towards his home, carrying a feeling of abject terror and despair at this new finding. Running through his mind like a whipping gale was the strange behaviour of Bodkin, his ready access to Society funds, Graham's observation of the double-counted expenses; and now, the looting of the account. To think! Bodkin, stealing like a thief, and likely enough for the benefit of that odious Father Whitechapel. "God forgive him," Loch murmured; "God forgive him," again and again, all the while envisioning in his mind's eye, clear as transparency, the devastating calamity looming ever closer.

Voice Behind the Door

EMBEZZLEMENT OF CHARITY FUNDS.
Considerable interest has been excited by a claim
brought before the Metropolitan police by Mr. H.
Howgrave Graham, assistant organising secretary of
the Charity Organisation Society. Geoffrey Bodkin,
Esq., treasurer of the Society, is suspected of fraudu-
lently taking and placing to his own use certain
moneys of the organisation, amounting to at least
£3,000. The defalcation is believed to have been covered by an ingenious manipulation of the figures and
divers false entries in the books. Mr. Bodkin is a
partner of Coutts & Co., but has been on sick-leave
recently. *The Times.* March 9, 1889.

LETTER AFTER LETTER WENT to Bodkin from Mr.
Loch, describing the unpleasant episode at the bank,
alerting the banker that the shortfall was discovered,
demanding an explanation and the replacing of the missing
money; and yet only silence, and still the more silence; until
Saturday morning came and Loch awoke to the dispiriting
article, as well as a mailbox brimming with angry letters from
fellow council members and prominent subscribers of the
Society. And thus Mr. Loch, with no little desperation, betook
himself to Mr. Bodkin's, nerving himself to finally have an
answer to this shameful business.

By the time the secretary arrived at the house, the court was very cool and a little damp, and full of premature twilight, the sky high up overhead dimming with the sunset. Spencer was taking inventory of the napery when the bell sounded, and seemed surprised to find the secretary at the door. "Bless me, sir, I was not expecting any visitors to-night," the butler greeted him. "The master is ill, and not seeing any one."

"So I have heard," Mr. Loch sighed. "However, I am afraid that there is a serious problem at hand, and much as I desire to abide your master's wishes, I must see him at once."

"Forgive me, sir," the butler apologised, "but that is impossible. You know the master's ways, and how he shuts himself up in the cabinet. I don't like it either—I may die if I like it—but sir, what can I do?"

Hearing this, Loch asked if he might sit down to have a word, and the butler took the secretary's hat and greatcoat as they traversed a large, low-roofed, comfortable hall, paved with flags, and warmed (after the fashion of a country house) by a bright fire behind a tall fender. This hallway had long been decorated with several tasteful and valuable pictures, pet fancies of Mr. Loch, although he noticed tonight, with some sense of added alarm, that the walls were blank.

Once seated at the dining table, Loch sighed heavily and resumed. "The truth, Spencer, is that there may have been some foul play at the bank; but your master perhaps can rectify the situation—if only he will talk to me. It is for his own good; otherwise, it will not only be myself to come round with questions." This last remark was made in a harsh, broken voice, in part from Loch's distress, but also to impress upon the butler the full import of the situation.

"Foul play?" cried the butler, his appearance altering for the worse at the tone of the visitor, whom he would not now look in the face. "Pray tell, what does sir mean?"

"I suppose, then," Mr. Loch answered, taking from his vest pocket the issue, "that you've not seen today's newspaper?"

"No, sir," replied the butler. "I have been busy all day, running errands for the master."

And here, much as it pained him to do so, the secretary laid upon the table the edition, and directed Spencer's eye to the offending article. Once finished reading, the latter rose to make a few nervous paces, his face white and eyes wide with alarm. After a moment, he mopped his brow with a red handkerchief; then, in a tone of strangled anguish: "Well, sir, this sounds very dire, but then again, this entire week has been rather"—the butler struggled for the word—"irregular."

"Now, Spencer," said Loch, "What do you mean by that? Is the master very ill?"

"I don't know, sir!" Spencer cried out, with a sudden splutter of emotion. "Master left off speaking since eight days ago."

"Your master has not spoken in eight days?" Loch asked. "How that?"

"Well, Mr. Loch, I'll explain," said Spencer. "All this last week, the master has been communicating only by notes. That is, he writes orders on a sheet of paper and throws it on the stair. This was never the master's way, yet I've had nothing else this week, nothing but papers and a closed door, the meals left there to be smuggled in when nobody was looking. But still, sir, every day, ay, and twice and thrice in the same day, there has been orders and complaints, strange ones: I am sent flying, every moment, east and west, to churches and chemists."

"Churches and chemists?" Loch repeated, deeply perplexed. "What does Bodkin want from them?"

Spencer shook his head sadly. "It is strange, sir, to talk of it. The master appears to be making rather generous donations of clothing, furniture and art, to parishes in the East End. I am to leave the things at the chapel door before sunrise and then go away. And yet…"

"Hm? And yet what?" Loch prompted, feeling sure of the underlying culprit.

"Well," the butler resumed—though he looked round him and began to whisper—"for all his giving things away, there appears to be some problem at the chemists with master's credit; and yet note after note comes, insisting upon the same firms, again and again, to send him certain salts and tinctures."

"Have you any of these papers?" asked the secretary.

Spencer felt in his pocket and handed out a crumpled note, which the secretary, bending nearer to the candle, carefully examined. Its contents ran thus:

"Mr. Bodkin presents his compliments to Mssrs. Evans. In December of 1888, Mr. B. received a somewhat large quantity from your firm. He assures them payment in full is forthcoming and now begs them to forward a similar order, credited to the same account. Terms of interest are no consideration. The importance of this to Mr. B. can hardly be exaggerated. FOR GOD'S SAKE SEND ME THE STUFF YOU WILL GET YOUR MONEY SOON

"This is a strange note," said Mr. Loch, "very unseemly"; and then, sharply: "How did you come to have it open?"

"The man at Evans's was main angry, sir, and he threw it back at me like so much dirt," returned Spencer.

Mr. Loch reflected on this for some moments, his musings growing darker, and then he demanded to speak to Mr. Bodkin at once, or at least make all attempt to do so; he would not leave the house otherwise.

"Well," said the butler, a muddle of fear and relief present in his face, "come along then to the cabinet door, and see if master will listen."

Mr. Loch followed Spencer into the hall, gay with firelight. "Are the rest of the servants to bed?" he inquired.

"All except Bradley," replied Spencer, referring to the footman. "But he is outside, locking up for the night."

"Very well," said Mr. Loch, reaching for the candle Spencer had lighted; then the men proceeded through the back garden and into the laboratory building, from which Bodkin's private cabinet was most conveniently entered. The far greater proportion of the building was occupied by the theatre, which filled almost the whole ground story and was lighted from above, and by the cabinet, which formed an upper story at one end and looked upon the court. A corridor joined the theatre to the door on the by-street, and with this the cabinet communicated separately by a second flight of stairs.

Here Spencer paused and lighted the way for Mr. Loch, who mounted the steps; then, making a great and obvious call on his resolution, he knocked with a somewhat uncertain hand on the red baize of the cabinet door. "Bodkin," he called, "this is Loch. I am sorry to intrude, but I must speak to you, to-night. I believe you know the matter at stake."

A voice answered from within: "I cannot see anyone," it said, mournfully.

At the sound of this reply, the secretary jolted and then scuttled out of earshot of the door, violently signing to the butler to follow him back across the yard and into the great kitchen, where the fire was out and the beetles were leaping on the floor. "Spencer," Mr. Loch said, a chilling hunch creeping into his thoughts, "was that your master's voice?"

"It seems much changed," replied the butler, with an answering horror in his eyes. "Ay, sir, I felt in my heart that something was out of sorts, but this, Mr. Loch, this is a thing that cries to Heaven!"

Loch now gathered the balance of his resolve and faced the butler squarely. "Spencer, have you ever seen in the house one called Father Whitechapel?"

The butler looked back at Mr. Loch in genuine bewilderment. "Father Whitechapel?" he repeated. "The man in the papers? Never, sir. Since my time."

"You are certain on this?" the secretary pressed, giving look for look. "He has not dined here?"

"*Dined* here? Not a once," the butler responded, though he halted with a sudden recognisance of something.

"What is it?" Mr. Loch barked. "Speak, man!"

Spencer beckoned Mr. Loch closer and spoke in a hushed tone. "Two days ago, sir, one of the housemaids came to me, claiming that she had seen Father Whitechapel in the cabinet."

"Indeed?" said the secretary. "What did you do about this?"

"Why, sir, I took it as foolishness," Spencer returned, again mopping his brow. "Mr. Bodkin would never allow Father Whitechapel to stay in his cabinet, when the city is searching up and down for him. You know the master's standing in London, sir. It doesn't hold water."

Loch gave pause here, realising Bodkin's extreme secrecy on the matter of Father Whitechapel, even with his most trusted staff. "That is well said, Spencer, and a mystery in itself. But considering the situation at hand, I may as well tell you that your master has been of late something of a patron to this Father Whitechapel. I know this for a fact." Spencer made no reply, and Loch continued dolefully: "Ay, for some time I have felt that evil was sure to come of that friendship. Consider, Spencer, that since your master began associating with that charlatan, poor Geoffrey has become an inscrutable recluse, a wealthy man now refused credit."

To this the butler only continued to stand dumbly; and Mr. Loch went on: "Perhaps, Spencer, you might send for the maid, so she can tell me what she saw. Please make haste about it."

The young woman came at the summons, turning very white and nervous when she saw the grim looks of the two men. "Put yourself together, Florence," said the butler. "Master may be in a position of some danger, and Mr. Loch here wants to ask you about what you saw in the cabinet this week."

"Well, sir, it was only once, and so quick, that I could hardly swear to anything," the maid began narrating, gathering her breath and clutching at her crucifix. "I came suddenly into the theatre from the garden. It seems the master had slipped outside for whatever reason, for the cabinet door was open, and there he was at the far end of the room digging among the crates. He looked up when I came in, gave a kind of whimper, and whipped upstairs into the cabinet. It was but for one brief moment that I saw, but indeed, what I saw did not look like my master; it was not of the same bigness. The master has a strong, husky build, and this person I saw was more of a beanpole, very light in step, and with quite a graceful way about him."

The secretary nodded curtly. "And how did you come to think the man was Father Whitechapel? You have met him before?"

"Yes, sir," she answered, with a look of awe and devotion. "When I was visiting my friend in Spitalfields."

"You do know that the man is wanted for murder?" Mr. Loch asked.

Suddenly the maid began to cry, and through her sobs looked up at her questioner. "I don't know, sir, if you ever met him yourself?"

"Yes," said the secretary, "I once spoke with him."

"Then you must know, sir," she hiccoughed; "that it is impossible for that gentleman to cause any harm to the master, or any other." The maid sighed in such a manner that was somewhat theatrical to the eye, and yet appeared to reflect true feeling. "I don't know rightly how to say it, sir, I'm not book-learned, but I give you my Bible-word, when I met him, I felt in my bones as though I were gazing upon a saint."

With this, the maid was dismissed back to her quarters, and the two men continued their conversation. "I fear, Spencer, that she speaks the truth," said Mr. Loch. "That was never Mr. Bodkin she saw outside the cabinet."

"But you see, sir, why I doubted," Spencer relayed, rather sulkily. "She speaks of that person rather oddly, does she not?"

"Quite so, but having met Father Whitechapel myself, I own I felt something of what she described," begrudged Mr. Loch. "The man, no doubt, has a certain charm."

"Well, he must do," the butler mused, "to put someone like the master under such a spell."

"But we must be logical about this, Spencer," Loch resumed. "Much as I am puzzled by the accounts which allege Father Whitechapel to be harmless, he is still sought as a murderer, and here he creeps and hides in another man's house, fleeing on sight. Does an innocent man act so? Yes, it all adds up: your master, Spencer, is being drugged and held hostage by Father Whitechapel, likely for reasons of extortion! Hence the alien voice from the cabinet; hence the avoidance of his friends and absence from the bank; hence the donations and chemicals; hence Bodkin's willingness to thieve and lie, and ruin himself completely—God grant that he is still alive! There is my explanation; it is bad enough, Spencer, ay, and appalling to consider, but it hangs well together; and makes plain and natural that some drastic action be taken."

The butler blanched and wilted at this speech, but made no protest. "As you say, sir," he returned, hoarsely. "I believe you, truly, but now comes the question, sir: what to do about it?"

Mr. Loch spent a moment in deep contemplation. "Well, Spencer, this is beyond me. Come what may, I must go and send for the police. I shall hope to be back shortly, but until then, say nothing to the man in the cabinet, lest he flee."

"Sir," Spencer nodded.

Then, leaving the stupefied butler by the fire in the hall, Mr. Loch departed Bodkin's house and sped for the Metropolitan police-station, his carriage bouncing along the serried points of gas-light that just barely pierced the blurry dusk of London.

In the Laboratory

IT WAS NIGH ON TEN O'CLOCK when Mr. Loch returned to Bodkin's estate, accompanied by Police-sergeant Golding and a young deputy. Golding was a hard man to satisfy, and the secretary had used some time at the station overcoming the sergeant's incredulity at the alleged connexion between Bodkin and Father Whitechapel. Yet finally Loch's insistence swayed him, and now there was even ambition in the officer's eyes, that the police might recover some esteem lost by thus far producing no viable suspect for the Ripper murders.

"Is that you again, Mr. Loch?" said Spencer, to the quiet tapping at the front door.

"It's all right," the secretary answered. "I have the police here. Open the door."

The butler admitted them swiftly, and the men moved in a body down the hall, until reaching the hearth, where huddled about like sheep was the whole of the servants, men and women. "What? You're all here?" Mr. Loch asked, with a ferocity of accent that testified to his own jangled nerves. Then, turning to Spencer: "I would think, for your master's sake, you would not call for an audience."

"Sir," the other countered, "it could not be helped."

Suddenly, the housemaid with whom he had conversed earlier ran toward Mr. Loch, and lifted up her voice. "Bless

God! He is innocent!" she cried, and clutched onto the secretary, pouring her wails into his breast as he wriggled from her grasp.

"Hold your tongue, girl!" Sgt. Golding snapped, taking the maid by her arm and roughly leading her back to the flock of house-staff. "We have serious business here, and we'll have no more of that."

Spencer directed his staff back to their quarters and returned to the men, who were discussing the plan of attack.

"We will give short warning," Golding was saying to the deputy. "And if anything seems amiss, I shall break in the cabinet door. Meanwhile, lest anyone seek to escape by the back, you go round the corner and stand post at the laboratory door. I give you ten minutes to get to your station."

"Ah, sir, that's talking," said Spencer. "There is an axe in the theatre"; and then, looking at Mr. Loch: "you might take the kitchen poker for yourself."

The secretary took that rude but weighty instrument into his hand, balanced it under his arm, and led the way into the yard. It was a wild, warm, seasonable night with a pale moon, lying on her back as though the biting east wind had tilted her, and a flying wrack of the most diaphanous and lawny texture. When they got there, the court was all full of wind and dust, and the thin trees in the garden were lashing themselves along the railing. The wind made talking difficult, flecked the blood into the face, and tossed the light of the candle to and fro about their steps, until they came into the shelter of the theatre.

As they drew nearer to the cabinet door, Sgt. Golding leaned forward, straining to hear from inside. "You are certain that is not Bodkin?" he asked the butler.

Both Spencer and Mr. Loch craned their necks to listen to the sounds of footfall moving to and fro along the cabinet floor. The steps fell lightly and oddly, with a certain swing, for all they went so swiftly; it was different indeed from the heavy creaking tread of Geoffrey Bodkin. "That is not the master's foot," Spencer mouthed.

"No, I don't suppose it is," confirmed the secretary in similar fashion, inching even further toward the door, till his ear was nearly pressed against the wood. "And—what now? Do you hear that?"

Drawing back from the door on tiptoe, the three men looked at each other, as though conscious of an extraordinary event taking place. "It sounds like weeping, does it not?" Golding whispered. "Almost like a woman."

"I have heard that same weeping over the week," the butler described. "Sometimes well into the night, along with the pacing."

"It's an ill conscience that's such an enemy to rest," Mr. Loch intoned, "and a good man foully used in every step."

But now the ten minutes drew to an end. Spencer disinterred the axe from under a stack of packing straw; the candle was set upon the nearest table to light them to the attack; and they again drew near to where that patient foot was still going up and down, up and down, in the quiet of the night.

"Geoffrey Bodkin, or whoever that is," the officer suddenly announced in a loud voice: "This is the Metropolitan police, demanding you open the door immediately." He paused a moment, but there came no reply. "I have given you fair warning," he continued, "and now I say again, you will open this door, or I will break it down!"

"For God's sake, brother," moaned the voice, "have mercy!"

"Ah, that's not Bodkin—it's Father Whitechapel!" exclaimed Loch. "Down with the door, sergeant!"

Golding swung the axe over his shoulder; the blow shook the building, and the red baize door leaped against the lock and hinges. Up went the axe again, and again the panels crashed and the frame bounded; four times the blow fell; but the door was very strong, the wood tough and the fittings of excellent workmanship; and it was not until the fifth, that the lock burst in sunder and the wreck of the door fell inwards on the carpet. The besiegers, appalled by their own riot and the stillness that had succeeded, stood back a little and peered in. There lay the cabinet before their eyes in the quiet lamplight, a good fire glowing and chattering on the hearth, the kettle singing its thin strain, a drawer or two open, papers set forth on the business-table, and nearer the fire, the things laid out for tea: the quietest room, you would have said, and but for the glazed presses full of chemicals, the most commonplace that night in London.

Right in the midst there sat on a small chair Father Whitechapel, calm as could be, his mouth slightly open; his mood receptive; a look upon his face of one suffering spiritual influence. The secretary, sergeant and butler stared upon the still figure for a long moment, the belligerence withering from their faces, for even among this chaos and violence, their quarry's blissful expression and beatific aura radiated like a fire in a forest.

"You are Father Whitechapel?" Golding asked firmly, the broken silence causing Loch and Spencer to jump.

"So it is said, brother," the sitting figure replied, his gentle voice unravelling like a silken scarf. He was wearing simple black pants and a black shirt, and the secretary could not help but to be struck again by the figure's remarkable combination of great authority and great apparent frailty of constitution.

"Where is Mr. Bodkin?" the sergeant pressed.

"Forgive me, brother, I cannot bring him back to you," Father Whitechapel answered, with a mien so disconsolate it brought a chill to the atmosphere.

"And Rose Millett?" Golding further demanded. "Did you murder the girl?"

"Ay, brother," Father Whitechapel returned.

This answer halted Golding, who now eyed the man in the chair as though a rare botanical specimen; yet he recalled himself, directing Spencer to fetch the deputy, and while the butler did so, the sergeant brought forth a pair of Hiatt cuffs. "I'll need to put these on you," he murmured.

The hostage nodded, silently offering his wrists to be bound.

Once the deputy returned to the cabinet, he led Father Whitechapel back through the house, with Mr. Loch following. Reaching the hallway, that same housemaid was there, and when she beheld the fair face of Father Whitechapel, and the shackles round his wrists, she immediately fell into an hysteria, throwing herself at the captive's ankles; and there she clung, kissing his feet and screaming, so that Loch thought all London would hear, of the injustice of this arrest.

Father Whitechapel merely smiled down upon the girl; the footman had literally to pry the maid away, and Loch clasp the writhing girl and fend off her blows, until Father Whitechapel was tucked into the cab and driven to the station by the deputy.

It was only under threat of a thrashing from Bradley that the maid fled tearfully back to her quarters; and Mr. Loch, breathing heavily from the exertion, returned back to the

cabinet, where he found Spencer and Sgt. Golding, still looking very mystified.

"Well," Mr. Loch said, breaking the trance, "the imposter is
gone to his account."

"And a strange imposter indeed," Golding answered.
"That's the man supposed to be going around killing? He
don't seem a likely character."

Mr. Loch and the officer exchanged glances. "Perhaps not,"
the former acknowledged, "but men have strange sides."

The three of them reposed on this for a moment, until the
sergeant shook himself out of the reverie. "Well, it still remains for us to find the body of Mr. Bodkin, if we are to
charge Father Whitechapel for the murder."

They began to rummage through the surgical theatre, with
its lumber of crates and bottles, its few dark closets and a spacious cellar. All these they now thoroughly examined. Each
closet needed but a glance, for all were empty, and all, by the
dust that fell from their doors, had stood long unopened. The
cellar was filled with crazy lumber, dating from the times of
the doctor who was Bodkin's predecessor, or even earlier; but
as they opened the door they were advertised of the uselessness of further search, by the fall of a perfect mat of cobweb
sealing the entrance. Nowhere was there any trace of Geoffrey
Bodkin, dead or alive.

Spencer stamped on the flags of the corridor. "He must be
buried here," he said, hearkening to the sound.

"Or he may have fled," said Loch, and he turned to examine the door in the by-street. It was locked, and lying nearby
on the flags, they found the key, already stained with rust.

"This does not look like use," observed the sergeant. "In
fact it looks as though a man had stamped on it till broken."

"Ay," continued Loch, "and the fractures, too, are rusty." The men looked at each other with a scare, then mounted the stair in silence, and still with an occasional awe-struck glance, proceeded more thoroughly to examine the contents of the cabinet. At one table, there were various dustings of some white salt on glass saucers, as though for a disrupted experiment, presumably with the chemicals Spencer had been unexplainably ordered to procure for Bodkin.

In the course of their review of the chamber, the searchers now divided, the sergeant heading toward Bodkin's business table, and Loch and the butler coming to a mirror in the style of a cheval-glass, so tilted as to show them nothing in its reflection but the rosy glow playing on the roof, the fire sparkling in a hundred repetitions along the glazed front of the presses, and their own pale and fearful countenances stooping to look in.

"What could Bodkin want with this?" Loch asked.

"I cannot say," whispered the butler, "but it has seen some strange things, sir."

"Pardon me, sirs," called Sgt. Golding from the other side of the room, "but I think you should look here."

This brought Loch and Spencer to the business table, atop of which was a cluttered array of startling papers, including a declaration of bankruptcy and a statement of outstanding debts; but most shocking was a notice, dated a week ago, of impending foreclosure and public auction of Bodkin's grand home.

"Good God," the officer remarked, with something of a gleam in his eye; "this is Bodkin of Coutts's? That's an end to come to, isn't it?"

Mr. Loch looked at Spencer, and then back at the paper. "Ay," lamented Loch, "I suspected troubles, God knows, but not such dire catastrophe! This has disgrace writ through and through."

"Look at this, sirs," Spencer offered, stooping over a table beside the tea-things and squinting down at a pile of bank cheques, which were scrawled, in Bodkin's own hand, with impossible sums and payable to various poor hospitals and salvation societies. "This cheque is dated today."

Mr. Loch swept up the cheque and confirmed as much. "So, then," he expounded, excitedly, "Bodkin was alive and here so recently! He cannot have been disposed of in so short a space. He must be still alive; he must have fled!" Mr. Loch turned toward the sergeant, as though for an explanation, but there was only a befuddled look in the latter's eyes.

"This is rather bizarre," Golding said, as the men went out of the theatre, locking the door behind them. "Perhaps the detectives can make better hand of the situation."

"Let us hope, too," the secretary added, "that we can keep this as quiet as possible."

"We will do our best," the officer replied, "but it may be too late." Then, ordering Mr. Loch and Spencer not to disturb anything in the cabinet, Sgt. Golding made his way from the house, still with the echo of the wailing maid ringing from inside.

EVENING NEWS
FRIDAY, APRIL 3, 1889

SHOCKING PLEA IN EAST-END MURDER CASE.

SLUM SAVIOUR "FATHER WHITECHAPEL" CONFESSES AS RIPPER.

DEATH SENTENCE PASSED IN LONDON.

Father Whitechapel (*alias*), of undetermined age and origin, who was indicted at the London Assizes yesterday for the wilful murder of Rose Millett, 29, at Clarkeyard, Poplar High-street, on December 22 of the past year, persisted in his plea of "Guilty," and was sentenced to death.

This same man has confessed as being "The Ripper" and causing the dreadful deaths of five prostitutes in the East-end. The confession, the truth of which remains to be established, was made to Scotland-yard officials, which proclaimed success in the capture of London's most notorious villain, who decoyed fallen women by almsgiving and then brutally murdered them.

The excitement to-day in London is intense, and the scene in the town this morning shows that the interest in the trial was even greater than had been anticipated. Soon after dawn this morning all the roads leading to the court-house were crowded with people coming in from the surrounding districts. Hours before the opening of the proceedings a large crowd, mainly composed of women, gathered in front of the court-house, and the street presented the appearance of being covered with a long awning of umbrellas. The constables were afraid to open the doors, but stood in the windows above and shouted to the crowd below ordering them away and threatening them with arrest if they did not disperse.

It was nearly 9 o'clock before the constables dared to open the doors to admit those having tickets. As they did so, masses of men and women pushed their way in with great violence. The constables were obliged to again shut the doors and then they alternately implored and threatened the crowd. Many women were severely crushed, and one or two fainted, but they would not retire, and finally the men gave way and permitted the ladies to enter. When at last the doors were opened the women fought like roughs for admission, and once inside they scampered madly to the front seats. The door was then securely locked, and only persons possessing orders signed by THE JUDGE were admitted. About this time JUDGE B.L. TALBOT appeared, accompanied by a body of newspaper correspondents, and with great difficulty succeeded in passing through the crowd.

Just before 10 o'clock the prisoner, plainly and neatly attired in all black, entered the dock slowly, seeming quite unmoved in spite of the scrutinising way in which both men and women peered into his face as he passed. All were firmly bent upon glimpsing the man, and every one sat as if riveted to their seats, gazing at the prisoner in the dock.

Asked by the Clerk if he had anyone appearing for him the accused replied in the negative.

When the Clerk of Arraigns read the indictment and asked Father Whitechapel to plead, the latter replied "Guilty."

The following is the confession:—"It was I that killed the child Rose, at Clarke's-yard, Poplar High-street, and the other poor women of the East-end. I make this confession because my soul is troubled by my crimes, and while I am alive I cannot sleep, nor can London. Now it is finished. I am ready to die for my crimes. I swear that this statement is true."

At this confession a gasp went up in the court-room, and several women had to be removed for causing too much commotion.

THE JUDGE said that the prisoner's role in the East-end murders, excepting Miss Millett, seems based upon a chain of circumstantial evidence as well as the anxiety of the police to claim a culprit for the murders; and he would only admit the plea of "Guilty" for the Millett crime, for in this case the prisoner was able to give a vivid and minute description of how the act was committed, and the position in which the body lay when completed, which corroborates with the coroner's report; further, there was an eyewitness account of Father Whitechapel being seen with the deceased on that night.

THE JUDGE.—Do you understand what it is you are pleading "Guilty" to?

Father Whitechapel.—Yes, brother.

THE JUDGE.—You are pleading "Guilty" to the wilful murder of Miss Millett. Do you understand that?

Father W.C.—Ay, brother.

THE JUDGE called upon Dr. E.J. Shannon, medical officer at Newgate Prison. Dr. Shannon stated that the prisoner had been under his observation for the past thirty-six hours. His general conversation and conduct were quite extraordinary, but there was no indication of mental disease. Father Whitechapel was fit to plead.

THE JUDGE stated that in the absence of any evidence upon the depositions which would suggest insanity, and of any evidence given in that Court of insanity, he was bound to rule that the submission did not afford grounds for rejecting the pleas if he was satisfied that the accused understood what it was and adhered to it.

The Clerk asked the prisoner whether he desired to adhere to his plea of "Guilty."

Father W.C.—Yes, brother.

JUDGE.—Do you thoroughly understand what it is you are pleading "Guilty" to?

Father W.C.—Yes, brother.

You are pleading "Guilty" to the wilful murder of this girl.—Yes, brother.

You understand the plea you are making and what the consequences of that must be?—Yes, brother.

You have well considered it?—With all my heart, brother.

Mr. T. EASTHAM, appearing for the prosecution, said that in view of the plea which had been entered, he did not think he need state the facts of the case. This is a grievous disappointment to those ticketholders who expected to witness a long trial.

Father W.C. was asked by the Clerk whether he had anything to say why sentence should not be passed upon him. He replied: "Let it be so, brother; I do not resist you."

It was one of the shortest murder trials on record at this Court.

Throughout the course of the trial no further information was ascertained about the man's family, origin, proper name or station. Despite the JUDGE'S statement, the rumour soon swept through the court-room and to those outside that "Jack the Ripper" has been caught.

THE JUDGE then sentenced the prisoner to be hanged, the execution to take place in three Sundays in the Newgate gaol yard. "Father Whitechapel, you will be taken hence to the prison in which you were last confined and from there to a place of execution where you will be hanged by the neck until you are dead and thereafter your body buried within the precincts of the prison. May the Lord have mercy upon your soul."

CHAPLAIN.—Amen.

H.R. CAMERON, the governor of the gaol, has not decided as to a definite line of conduct in the management of the condemned's remaining days, but it is expected that he will be placed in solitary confinement and allowed no visitors, save the chaplain and prison-guards.

Remarkable Death of Father Whitechapel

COUTTS'S BANKER STILL MISSING.
The whereabouts have not been determined, nor has a body been recovered, for Mr. Geoffrey Bodkin, partner at Coutts & Co., bankers. Mr. Bodkin has been missing now for three weeks, and grave fears are entertained for his safety. The officials of the Criminal Investigation Department are at present actively endeavouring to discover some trace of the missing gentleman. Bodkin, former treasurer of the Charity Organisation Society, is charged with embezzling from the same. A warrant exists for his apprehension in connexion with the defalcations, and it is thought that he has absconded from the country or committed self-destruction. A representative from the C.I.D. stated: "It is not only an unsolved, but a perplexing mystery, which urges itself the more on attention from the shade of suspicion of crime which hangs over the matter. The case is one of an extraordinary character." Description of Mr. Bodkin, 43, is as follows: height 5ft. 10in.; square build; tanned complexion, brown hair divided to the left, moustache. *The Times*. April 8, 1889.

FOR THREE WEEKS THE SUBJECT of Father Whitechapel was foremost on London's mind; and the range of emotions attached to the confession and death-sentence was as vast as the human mind itself. There were those who had met with the kindness of the condemned man and proclaimed his guilt impossible; but so too, there were those who hurled hatred at such profound double-dealing as a murdering almsgiver. "Monster or saint?"—this was the question being whipped round London; and the division of opinion was largely along class lines, with the wealthier strata proclaiming relief at having such a troublemaker as Father Whitechapel cleared away; and the poorer people proclaiming the kindness of the latter and the shame of his persecution. And as the days passed, and the chance of a royal pardon became slimmer, the furore grew ever greater. Letters filled the boxes of Newgate Prison; daily there were wailing crowds at the gaol's boundary, trying in vain to be admitted; and in one extraordinary case, a young woman from the East End committed a rather serious crime in an attempt to be sent to prison and meet Father Whitechapel.

Inside the prison walls, the excitement was hardly different: the warders fought and bribed each other over who would be assigned watch-duty over Father Whitechapel; every bit of news was hurriedly sold to the papers; and personal effects of the prisoner's were snatched up to be auctioned to the throngs of weeping women at the gates. The thirst for new information or ripe rumour was so insatiable, in fact, that to meet the demand, enterprising writers hastily scribbled sensational articles and pamphlets about Father Whitechapel, the contents of which were largely and outright fabricated, and which ranged from describing the man as a veritable angel to Beelzebub incarnate, yet nonetheless sold out their editions with astounding celerity.

The man with more access to Father Whitechapel than anyone was Newgate's chaplain, the Reverend R. K. Berry; but for the dozens of questions daily put to him, he had little to report about the unvarying character of the prisoner's days. Father Whitechapel had entered the prison in silence and was led to his private cell, looking about him with such beaming goodness as made the warders quake in devotion. Even Cameron, the dour governor of the prison, was quite taken by the famed inmate and was pleased to serve him, although Father Whitechapel asked for no special privileges or comforts; only for wherewithal to write, which was happily supplied. It was reported, too, that Father Whitechapel preferred his own company; he rarely spoke except to offer passages from Scripture, and seemed neither to sleep nor eat, except a few bits of dry bread and water. He simply sat at his bench reading from a Bible, upon which he seemed to make copious notes, or gazed out the barred windows of his barren cell with a blissful, serene expression.

The condemned man allowed the chaplain to visit occasionally, although during these meetings Father Whitechapel merely sat silently, holding the clergyman's hand, and indeed, when the latter departed from these meetings, it was with a distinct feeling that it was the prisoner ministering to him, rather than the reverse. "Christ alone could match that man something," he remarked to himself one day, as he tottered from the cell with a warm tingling in his body. There was even a rumour going about that the chaplain and prison-governor had offered Father Whitechapel escape in the pitch of night; yet (so it was said) the latter refused this graciously, claiming obedience to the law and sentence passed.

Finally, when it seemed that London would break under the strain of anticipation, the day of the execution came. A week had passed since Father Whitechapel had been led to Newgate's chapel to hear the compulsory sermon and burial service for the Church of England; this had nearly led to a riot among the prisoners, for a chance to view Father Whitechapel; and now, at forty-five minutes past eight o'clock on this morning, the prison-governor entered the man's cell and informed that no mercy had been passed, and the final hour had come.

"So it has, brother," Father Whitechapel replied, a tranquil smile upon his pale face. "Will you allow me to hold the Good Book?"

"You may," Cameron answered, throatily. He called for the warders, who went about with leather straps, loosely pinioning Father Whitechapel for the short walk to the gallows. The group now met with the chaplain and prison-doctor, and all shuffled outside and across the yard, toward the thick black posts and dangling rope, nearby to which was an expectant grave. There was already a buzzing and crying public assembled outside the prison walls, and once the execution-bell began its tolling, the crowd grew louder, until the executioner nearly had to holler his instructions.

Marwood the hangman, London's grimmest professional, was well used to these events, which he conducted expeditiously and without a trace of emotion. Yet this morning, upon his first glimpse of Father Whitechapel, he looked over knowingly at the chaplain. "Quite as you say," the executioner murmured, but went on preparing the condemned for the long drop: fastening the pinions more tightly to draw Father Whitechapel's ankles together, and drawing the man to the chalk mark on the trap-door.

Throughout all this there stood watching from a modest distance an audience of three: the High Sheriff, one journalist who had fought the fight of his life for the privilege—and Mr. C. S. Loch, who by special invitation from the sheriff was serving as a witness. Over the past weeks the secretary had devoured the published accounts of Father Whitechapel, reflecting on the famous character; yet still Mr. Loch was besieged with questions about Bodkin's fantastical downfall and disappearance, and still toiling in darkness to comprehend its relation to Father Whitechapel's subsequent arrest and imprisonment.

It is one thing to mortify curiosity, however, and another to gratify it; and now, as Mr. Loch stood in the balmy morning, holding his hat down against the gusts, he began to feel a nausea and distaste of this morbid event. Despite his campaign against Father Whitechapel and the latter's open-handed charity; despite the prisoner's confession of murder; despite Loch's own spiritual scepticism—despite all this, the scene of this extraordinary figure docilely submitting to his execution prompted something of a religious stirring in that God-fearing, but not particularly devout Mr. Loch: it seemed incredible that the gentle-looking man on the scaffold, clutching a well-worn Bible, merited such a miserable fate. "Dear God," the secretary asked himself, "can this really happen?"

Father Whitechapel now beckoned for the prison-governor; and when the man came forward, the other held out the Bible in his hands as though in offering, then leaned forward and murmured something, at which point the governor stepped from the scaffold and approached Mr. Loch.

"You are Loch?" the governor asked, and when the secretary confirmed as much: "He wants me to give you this," returned the other, and placed the Bible-book in Mr. Loch's hands before retreating back toward the gallows.

It was now asked of Father Whitechapel if he had any last statement. "Brothers," he intoned, his eyes lifted toward the sky, "he has dispersed; he has given to the poor; his righteousness endures for ever; his horn shall be exalted with honour."

The words were simple and characteristic in their citing of the Psalms, but nonetheless struck all in attendance as highly affecting; the chaplain was openly sobbing and even the executioner gave a stout gulp before draping the thick noose over Father Whitechapel's head and adjusting the knot, leaving the free rope to run down his slender back.

At this time the robed chaplain began the final prayers, a long and fervent invocation for God's mercy upon the condemned. As the recitation continued, Mr. Loch glanced down at the leather-clad book, baffled as to why the prisoner would single him out to receive it—but when he opened the book to a random page, Loch's spine turned to ice and his hair stood on end like quills.

The Bible-book had been heavily annotated; indeed, as Loch frantically flipped the delicate pages, he saw that it had been used as a makeshift diary, with large, bold script overriding the fine, faded print of the verses:

...forgive me! Forgive me, Rose! Forgive me, Charles! Forgive me, London! O, how I have failed of what I hoped! How I have tottered and stumbled! How I have debased myself...

Loch staggered, swooned and groped about like a man dizzy from blows, his mind submerged in shock—for the hand-of-write was unmistakably that of Geoffrey Bodkin.

Now there was a moment of silence during which the low, thick clouds shifted to shield all traces of sunlight from the gaol-yard. "Halt! Halt!" Mr. Loch shouted, but in vain, for

Marwood quickly stepped to the side and pulled the lever, sending Father Whitechapel plummeting down with a terrible thud, as the black flag was hoisted on the pole near the main gate and rending wails from the gathering throngs rose up to split the fog.

The hanged victim jerked violently and the neck snapped upward, but death was not instantaneous. Suddenly there came a change in the contorted and twitching man. From his wide-opened mouth came a dismal wail as of a banshee; he seemed to swell; his face became suddenly black; the features melted and altered into an amorphous and wildly gesticulating dust. The surrounding men sprang back; the sheriff raised his arm to shield himself from that sight; and the gallows shook and rattled as though they would collapse under the violent convulsing of the victim.

"O God!" Loch screamed, and "O God!" again and again, as the spasms diminished; but now Father Whitechapel was no more to be seen, and in his place, hanged from the noose, the cords of his face still moving with a semblance of life, but life quite gone; there, swaying gently in the cool morning air—was Geoffrey Bodkin!

The Full Confession of Geoffrey Bodkin

I WAS BORN IN THE YEAR 1843 to a comfortable family; endowed besides with excellent parts, businesslike by nature, fond of the respect of the wealthy and titled among my fellowmen, possessing the manners and accomplishments of a gentleman, and thus, as might have been supposed, with every guarantee of a respectable and lucrative future. My mother being a pious Christian, her own hope for me was a life of the cloth, but my father's wishes won out over his meeker wife, and I therefore followed in his distinguished footsteps at Coutts's bank, progressing infallibly in one direction and in one direction only: that of my career, which by its very nature demanded a more than commonly callousness of soul. Yet the bloodline of my kind-hearted mother could not be wholly stamped out, and while nurturing my reputation as London's most merciless dealmaker, I was aware of a certain secret sympathy for the downtrodden, which I found hard to reconcile with my imperious desire to conduct myself in the interests of the bank.

No surprise, then, that my work reacted to and shed a strong light on my consciousness of this perennial war among my members. I would be sympathetically disposed at times to tales of appalling poverty, but as my covert sentiments were, to say the least, incompatible with those of my clients, and I was not only highly-placed at the bank and well-considered by its directors, but also at an age where eccentricity was much frowned upon, this internal conflict of pragmatism and mercy grew ever more unwelcome. Many a man would have easily pardoned, even embraced the soft-heartedness I was guilty of; but from the acquisitive profession I was bound to, I hid it with an almost morbid sense of shame. Amongst moneyed men I was looked to as an oracle, but the more my livelihood flourished, the more I concealed my guilty conscience, and when I reached years of reflection and began to take stock of my progress and position in the world, I realised that I stood committed to a profound duplicity of life.

In my case, I was driven to reflect upon that hard law of *laissez-faire*, which lay deeply and inveterately at the root of my work and is yet one of the most plentiful springs of distress. By light of day, I laboured on behalf of my well-heeled clients, punctual to an extreme in the discharge of my duties; yet in the evenings, reposing in the Book of Books and reflecting on His words, I would ache for London's poor, promising subsequent penitence—but not quite moved to active goodwill, and soon enough lulled back into complacency by the comforts of privilege and wealth. After all, I reflected, I was no worse than other gentlemen; the division of capital and labour was inevitable and unchangeable; and what was more, I was only doing my part to bolster London's economy and thereby serve my country. Yet with each passing year and new promotion, I grappled ever more with the rights and wrongs of my situation, from both the moral and the intellectual sides of my intelligence—until came that fateful discovery by which my life was altered at once and forever.

II

I had acquired my house from the estate of a well-known doctor, and still occupying a large section of the property was a medical theatre with myriad chemical apparatus. All of this was quite useless to me, however (except as a bargaining chip), and once settled in, I began reverting the wing back to a garden. But upon removal of the floorboards, the labourers came to me with a smallish metal lock-fast box, now unlocked and, I supposed, already relieved of any material treasure.

Examining the remaining contents, upon first glance I was disappointed: handwritten papers, some of which appeared to be ingredient lists of some chemical admixture, along with an ordinary version-book containing scribbled instructions and a series of dates. These were arranged in the style of a ledger, with a brief remark occasionally appended to a date, usually no more than a digit or a single word: "triple," for instance, which occurred perhaps six times; and once later down the list and followed by several marks of exclamation, "failed!!!"

All this, though it whetted my curiosity, told me little that was definite. Nevertheless, intrigued as to why the papers merited such a burial, I sat down by the light of a melancholy candle and began to read. Here, it seemed, was a series of philosophical ramblings by the late doctor, curiously enough, rather in line with my own prolonged musings. Thus he wrote (and you shall pardon me to transpose his own words) of the duality of man, of two selves contending in the field of consciousness, and, of the two, man being rightly neither for being radically both.

I plunged deeper, the author's tale gone home in me; and saw that the doctor had far outstripped me, hazarding ideas of the separation of these elements. That these incongruous denizens are bound together is the curse of man, the late doctor postulated; yet could they be housed in separate identities, life might be relieved of all that was unbearable.

This daydream struck me profoundly. Think of it! The heartless banker might go his own way, holding his position securely and reaping the rewards, delivered from the longings and remorse of his more upright twin; and my second self could walk steadfastly on his unselfish path, doing his noble and altruistic things, no longer exposed to professional disgrace by the hands of this eccentric passion. Truly I could serve both God and Mammon. How, then, were these polar twins dissociated?

By excellent good fortune, the brittle papers offered a reply: the doctor, in the course of his experiments, had recognised the natural body for a mere manifestation of its spirits; further, he had discovered certain agents to have the power to sweep away that fleshy attire. But most dramatically, the doctor claimed to have compounded a drug by which the usual character of a man would be toppled and usurped by that which, till then, had remained confined and subservient. All of this suggested only the most naked possibility of a miracle, and coming to the final leaf of this strange document and shaking from my daze, I began to nurse my scepticism. It all seemed apocryphal—yet no doubt that certain stirrings occupied my thoughts.

I recalled the whispers of mystery surrounding the untimely death of that Dr. Jekyll; I thought of the ashen-faced lawyer, Utterson, who had handled the conveyancing in such foolhardy haste; the latter's subsequent removal from London; and I began indulging in the fantasy. It was not unheard of for a drug to alter someone's personality—why not divide it altogether? Has not the potter power to make of the same lump of clay one honourable vessel, and another dishonourable?

And here in my own hand rested the ingredients by which Jekyll's wild theory might be put to the test of practise.

III

Like a man possessed, I halted the dismantling of the laboratory and procured from a firm of wholesale chemists the necessary solution and the particular salt detailed in the notes. Yet still I wavered, for any drug that so potently transfigured one's identity might by the least accident of dosage or misstep in its formation annihilate it altogether. I knew well that I risked much: plausible enough that this very draught accounted for the doctor's own demise; but finally the temptation of a discovery so singular and profound at last overcame the suggestions of alarm; and late one accursed night, I measured out a glass of the blood-red liquor and added the powders.

The mixture, which was at first of a reddish hue and highly pungent to the sense of smell, began, in proportion as the crystals melted, to brighten in colour, effervesce audibly, and throw off small fumes of vapour. Suddenly and at the same moment, the ebullition ceased and the compound changed to a dark purple, which faded again more slowly to a watery green. When finally all subsided, I grasped the phial and, with a strong glow of courage, put the glass to my lips and drank at one gulp.

The most racking pangs succeeded: a grinding in the bones, deadly nausea, and a horror of the spirit that cannot be exceeded at the hour of birth or death. Then these agonies began swiftly to subside, and I came to myself as if out of a great sickness. There was something strange in my sensations, something indescribably new and, from its very novelty, incredibly sweet. I felt younger, lighter, brighter in body; within I was conscious of a heady recklessness, a current of sublime images running in my fancy, a solution of the bonds of obligation, an unknown and pristine innocence of the soul—and most of all, a perfect and effortless grasp of the Bible-word. I knew myself, at the first breath of this new life, to be more sympathetic, tenfold more sympathetic, sold a slave to my original compassion; and in that moment the thought braced and delighted me like wine. I stretched out my hands, exulting in the freshness of these sensations; and in the act, I was suddenly aware of the drastic change to my clay continent.

There was a tall cheval-glass in the laboratory quite suited to observing these transformations, and with trembling hands, I turned myself to the mirror and saw for the first time the appearance of Father Whitechapel. Now, while I consider myself book-learned enough, my grasp of metaphysics is rudimentary at best, and I must here speak not by my own theories but the doctor's, applying to my own situation what Jekyll had deemed most probable. In spite of my inward compunction, the outward course of Bodkin's life had been, after all, nine-tenths a life of greed, conceit, and connivance; the goodly side of my nature, which I had now transferred to the forefront, had been much less exercised, and therefore this side of myself was less robust and less developed than the predatory banker I had just deposed. Hence it came about that physically, Father Whitechapel was so much leaner and less matured than Geoffrey Bodkin; although from a moral standpoint, the movement was wholly upwards. Even as coldness shone upon the countenance of the one, true benevolence was written broadly and plainly on the face of the other.

Compassion besides (which we are taught is the best of man) had left on that body an imprint of innocence and fragility.

Yet when I looked upon that comely idol in the glass, I was conscious of no shock, but rather a leap of welcome. This, too, was myself. It seemed natural and human. In my eyes the creature bore a livelier image of the spirit, and seemed more express and single than the divided countenance I had been hitherto accustomed to call mine. And insofar I was doubtless right. I have observed that when I wore the semblance of Father Whitechapel, none could come near to me without a visible relaxing and warming of the flesh. This is because, given the close overlap of good and evil, and how circumstances modify propriety, all human beings, as we meet them, seem to be commingled out of good and evil—yet Father Whitechapel, alone in the ranks of mankind, was pure good.

But now there was the second and even more critical trial to be attempted. Though I had had no way of making sure my old identity would not be lost beyond redemption, the doctor's notes of his own experimentation intimated that re-administering the elixir would recall the character, stature, and face of Geoffrey Bodkin. Thus after lingering a few more moments at the mirror, mesmerised by my new reflection but praying for its impermanence, I once more prepared and drank the cup, once more suffered the pangs of dissolution, and to my untold relief, came to myself once more.

I now had two appearances to match my two characters: one altogether good, and the other still the old, mismatched compound of Geoffrey Bodkin, whose reformation and improvement I had already learned to despair of in the face of his brutal profession. All of that now seemed far in the past, however, and I went to sleep that night dreaming and smiling at my dreams, rejoicing in this shiny new persona, born to the world to save Bodkin from his sins.

IV

My prestigious career at Coutts's may have been the envy of countless upstarts, but still my success could not quite conquer my private aversions to serving as banker to London's wealthiest. In times of slack trade, when I was pressed to recommend savage labour cuts or price rises, my conscience would clang out ever more loudly; and when finally unable to ignore the peals, I would go forth late at night (in my usual form of Bodkin) to Mile-End Road, to buy my indulgences, laying aside restraint and frantically passing out coins to every beggar and tramp. These outings served as an opiate to my ailing sensibilities; yet upon my return home with my conscience quieted, I would then reflect on these handouts with some regret. What rank hypocrisy it seemed, to spend my days at Coutts's, conniving at and enriching my own self with gluttonous, manipulative dealings that brought sorrow and suffering to so many, and then giving the surplus of my gains to the very same victims of the slaughter. And just as problematical with these secret sallies was my fear of discovery. Should Bodkin be seen creeping around the East End at such ungodly hours, and emptying his pockets to boot, the scandal would destroy me. All would be lost: my position, my credit, truly, my life.

It was here, then, that the power of the potion continually tempted me. I had but to drink the cup to doff at once the body of the hard-hearted money-man, and to assume, like a thick cloak, that of Father Whitechapel. Bodkin could plod respectably in the public eye with a load of frugality and conservatism, but in a moment, like a schoolboy, strip off these bindings and spring headlong into a sea of liberality, reaping the spiritual spoils of charity while remaining wholly anonymous. I smiled at the notion; it seemed humorous at the time. After all—Father Whitechapel did not even exist! Let me escape into my laboratory door, give me but a second or two to mix and swallow the draught that I had always standing ready, and whatever he might have done, the kindly almsgiver would pass away like a story that is told; and there in his stead, quietly at home, studying his account-books, a man known as the clenched fist of Coutts's, would be Geoffrey Bodkin.

I lost little time in availing myself of my newfound immunity, although in these early days of my adventures, there was one mishap that piqued my concern and displayed a chink in what seemed my impenetrable mantle. A chance meeting of Father Whitechapel and a certain clergyman (whom I recognised in the person of Loch's walking companion) led to an impetuous act of generosity, whereby Father Whitechapel presumed to support a parish fund with a large cheque drawn in the name of Geoffrey Bodkin. This act not only threatened to expose the latter, but just as alarming, I began to spy the danger of allowing my new shape free rein upon my wherewithal. On my first journey to the East End, I had equipped Father Whitechapel with ten pounds in coin, expecting this to be sufficient for the evening—pah! The sum was spent in minutes. Indeed, his generosity knew no bounds; he would have gladly bankrupted Bodkin within days; and to eliminate such hazard, I converted a portion of my personal capital into cash and stored this in my laboratory, fortifying with the most studious care Bodkin's bank account from Father Whitechapel's magnanimous hands.

Now supposing myself safe from serious pecuniary loss, I went about further preparations, taking that sordid room in the Whitechapel district, where I secreted under the floorboards a large dose of the concoction, should the need arise; and on the other side, I breathed not a word of Father Whitechapel to my butler Spencer or his staff. My second character would be strictly confined to the cabinet and laboratory, I decided, and never permitted into the main wings of my home. With these precautions in place, I believed myself to be beyond the reach of fate, and henceforth released Father Whitechapel into the great city, where, on his part, he was immediately drawn as though by magnet to one specific place: that cancer of London's concealed disgrace, the East End of the East End—and *à propos*, his namesake.

V

The aid which I made haste to offer in my disguise was, at first, big-hearted; but in the hands of Father Whitechapel, it soon began to turn toward the saintly. When I would come back from these excursions, I could only wonder at my vicarious charity and sympathy that made my alter-ego more revered among the multitudes of those wretched streets than any clergyman, Salvationist, or night-nurse. "To them which sat in the region and shadow of death, a light had sprung up"—and Geoffrey Bodkin stood humbled to the dust, aghast before the loving acts of Father Whitechapel. This familiar that I called out of my own soul was a being inherently benign and tender; his every act and thought centred on others, helping them with pure generosity and to any degree of torture to himself; tolerant like a man of stone.

Into the minute details of the nightly aid that that alien prince thus proffered, I have no design of entering, though I will mention one aspect of my methodology. Of all the lost souls that Father Whitechapel met in the East End, none struck him as more needy of a shepherd as the young street-walkers who in their extreme want resorted to feeding themselves and their children on the proceeds of womanly shame. It was to these poor souls that my counterpart specially ministered, recording their names and locations in a small black book. This, of course, was during the height of the Ripper's carnage, and the grisly accounts in the papers only impelled Father Whitechapel to do all the more for the terrified women being swept away by the tide of complacency in upper-class London.

Yet if Father Whitechapel's love of and care for these forgotten women was inspiring, I should relate (while on the topic of the Ripper) one very peculiar and very spooking incident that served to show me the true depth of my double's compassion. It was a cold, black night in November, and Father Whitechapel was coming through a narrow alleyway, when suddenly at a short distance off he spotted a small, almost dwarfish man. This man seemed to be deformed somehow, or at least he emanated a strong feeling of deformity and decay; either way, something about the way he was chattering to himself and walking fast, as though hunted by fears, gave me strong suspicion; and when I glanced down and noticed that his heavy shoes dripped with blood, I could naught but believe that I was looking upon London's famed slayer. Now, in the eyes of all, this chap was one that nobody could have anything to do with, a really damnable man; if Father Whitechapel might hate any man or call him an enemy, it could be this one—and yet that being of unending and universal forgiveness was incapable of anything except love; no part of his thoughts even hinted at bitterness or punishment; he sought only to heal this sickly-looking malefactor, who now sobbed under the beam of Father Whitechapel.

"Come, brother," I spoke gently; "take my hand, so that your God in Heaven may forgive you"—yet the sinister man turned away and disappeared in the darkness, leaving Father Whitechapel alone to pray for the man's soul.

Sure enough, the next morning's paper reported the macabre death of the young, buxom woman I knew as "Fair Emma"; and but a day or two later, the paper reported another death, this one the suicide of an unidentified man, by way of gunshot. Bodkin read this while breakfasting, shaken to some degree, and with a definite inkling that it was the obituary of the bloody man from the alley.

Whether or not that person was, in actuality, London's Ripper, I suppose will never be known; yet shortly thereafter, the bloodbath seemed to peter out. Either way, I was pleased enough at this conclusion. For in that irony of ironies, that conformist Bodkin had balked at the idea of going to the police with information regarding that disturbing night, lest he risk connecting his own name with London's most heinous criminal—or its purest soul.

VI

During these first weeks of my existence as both Bodkin and Father Whitechapel, the partition between the two was starkly defined. No matter what the latter did in the East End under cover of night, Bodkin himself was no more liberal; he woke again to his prudent qualities seemingly unimpaired; and in fact he would even make haste, where it was possible, to balance out the profligate charity of Father Whitechapel by labouring all the more to safeguard what are regarded as natural disparities of class. But the compounding of time spent in my second person began to have a marked effect. My visits to the East End, and the amount of money passed out, escalated steadily, which alone should have served as warning of the possibility of catastrophe. Soon, though, I began to notice that even when outwardly Bodkin, I could feel my doppelgänger's presence inside of me, tortured with throes and longings, struggling to be free—and just as Bodkin lived vicariously through Father Whitechapel, the latter began to follow suit.

I had long been proud of my role as the Charity Society's Treasurer, grateful for the air of respectability it lent to both Bodkin's reputation and to the furtherance of his career. I did not wholly disagree with the Society's principles of self-help and organised giving, but since Father Whitechapel's arrival, I was increasingly dismayed by the old conflict that had stunk in the nostrils of the poor for so long: the discord between our sparing charity and the wasteful expenditures of the council. In that regard, I pored over our treasury reports as I would a balance-sheet, remarking upon the sixty and one-quarter per-cent of Society income absorbed by salaries, rent, printing, postage, and so forth; and thus guided by Father White-chapel's invisible hand, Bodkin carelessly penned that Society Addendum to call out his council for these gross superfluities and inequalities in their finances.

My efforts to redress these grievances were, to say the least, badly received at a noisy council meeting, which prompted me (again under guidance of my secret self) to plot a wily retribu-tion. Having access to the Society's infamous Applicant and Decision Book, I transcribed into Father Whitechapel's black book a list of those denied relief, so that he might visit and aid them. This alone was hardly criminal, but now with a healthy grudge and a mind swooning with frightful remembrances of poverty, I further proposed that if the Society would not of its own volition spend its money to help London's indigent— then Father Whitechapel would do it for them. Thus I conceived that gymnastic accountancy whereby I rerouted funds out of the Charity Society's coffers and into the hands of those pitiful rejects that seemed, at least to Father Whitechapel, to need help the very most of all.

I know that this ruse marks me the chief of sinners in the eyes of the Society council; indeed, Geoffrey Bodkin realised the dangerous course he was travelling, for as a rule misappropriation can last only so long, and the Society funds began draining more rapidly than anticipated. Yet my situation was apart from ordinary laws, and insidiously relaxed the grasp of propriety. It was *him*, after all, and him alone, that was responsible. Bodkin, on his part, could only plead helplessness under the subconscious meddling of Father Whitechapel, who day by day gathered more shares in our unique partnership.

VII

Some two months after Father Whitechapel's first appearance, I set out at my usual time (well past midnight), with one of the Society application tickets in hand. This applicant, one Rose Millett, was yet another courtesan, driven to sell herself and prone to easing her sorrows with drink. Looking at the rejected ticket, something in the description of the girl struck a note in me, but it was not until I found her and looked upon her face that I realised this was none other than "Drunken Lizzie" (the name by which I knew her)—one of the streetwalkers frequented at times by Geoffrey Bodkin. But dear

God! O, the pangs of remorse when now I confronted her as Father Whitechapel, that uncompromising force of purity and goodness! O, how I recalled the banker's sinful treatment of the young woman! Father Whitechapel could now not do enough for her; he poured out his perfect love; tended specially to her through the night; and, what was a first, allowed her to spend a chaste night with him in the lodging house.

We finally settled in to sleep at a late hour, and waking the next morning beside her, I was aware of a somewhat odd sensation. It was in vain I looked about me and saw the barren, slanted room in the lodging house, and recognised the bed of rags—yet something still kept insisting that I was not where I was, that I had not wakened where I seemed to be, but rather in the tall, decent room where I was accustomed to sleep in the body of Geoffrey Bodkin, among my mahogany-framed bed and my fine furniture.

I puzzled lazily about this illusion, until an impudent vermin jolted me and caused my eyes to fall upon my hand. Now the hand of Father Whitechapel was almost feminine in shape and size: it was slender, white, and delicate. But the hand which I now saw, clearly enough, by the yellow light of a nearby streetlamp, lying half shut on the floor, was large, corded, knuckly, of a dusky pallor and thickly shaded with a swart growth of hair. It was the hand of Geoffrey Bodkin.

I must have stared upon it for near half a minute, dumb with wonder, before an insurgent terror woke up in my breast, as sudden and startling as the crash of cymbals. Then, using my hands to feel the features of my face, my fears were realised. Yes, I had fallen asleep Father Whitechapel, and without aid of the drug, had reverted to Geoffrey Bodkin during my slumber. How was this to be explained? My mind reeled; the night was far gone into the morning; any moment now the sleeping Rose would rise, and soon after the lodging house would be up and about. For a man of my stature to be seen in this section of London, at this hour, implied the worst; and what was more, what could Rose make of dozing off beside Father Whitechapel, and awakening not only to a different man, but one that she might well recognise from previous trysts?

Though I recalled that emergency dose of the drug I had stored below the floorboards of the room, I could not now use it to don my mask, for prying up the box would certainly have roused my roommate from her slumber. Thus, with little other choice, I hastened away, ducking low and attempting to conceal my face. The moment I stepped outside I was accosted by two begging children; these I brushed aside and continued running, my blood changed into something exquisitely thin and icy, until with an overpowering sweetness of relief, a closed cab sped by, but would have passed on had I not thrown myself in front of it and held out a pound note. The driver halted, and I told him my destination in gasping breaths. "Gone slummin', eh?" he sneered down at me; but he let me up and accepted the note, blackmailing me for the change, and drove me to my home, where I entered through the laboratory door, terrified my servants would see me arriving home at such an hour and in such a state.

Once safely inside, I washed and dressed, and then sat down for breakfast. Small indeed was my appetite, however, as I began to reflect more seriously than ever before on the issues and possibilities of my double existence. Through my previous experience, I had noted that the power of the drug had not always been equally displayed; once it had totally failed to throw off the body of Bodkin; and since then I had been obliged to increase the doses, gradually but decidedly, until I was put on recent occasions (in line with the cryptic notes of the doctor) to double, and then, with alarming risk, to treble the amount. It was not only these uncertainties that cast a shadow on my contentment; it further appeared that despite my larger dosing, that saintly part of me which I had the power of projecting had lately been in ascendancy for shorter and shorter duration, though till now always long enough to allow me to return to my cabinet, with time to spare.

Now, however, this morning's accident seemed, like the Babylonian finger on the wall, to be spelling out my destiny. All things therefore seemed to point to this: my tolerance for the drug markedly increased, I was slowly losing hold of my hitherto impervious disguise; and that by prolonging this masquerade, I risked serious damage to my original self, Bodkin, whose professional stature, while seemingly secure, was yet so precarious by its elevated nature.

VIII

With my rude awakening in the Whitechapel lodging house, and the growing turbulence of my double life, I now felt I had to choose between my two selves. My two natures had memory in common, but all other faculties were most unequally shared between them. Bodkin (who was composite), now with pitiless dealings, now with a guilty conscience, projected and shared in the warm glow of Father Whitechapel; but the latter was pitying of Bodkin, believing him a misguided bandit in pursuit of fool's gold. Alas! So much hung in the balance. Bodkin, the stern patriarch, had infinitely more interest in propriety, comfort and luxury; Father Whitechapel, however, completely indifferent to accumulation or appearances, would have been delighted to heave off the mean banker and sacrifice everything for the sake of London's submerged.

Strange as my circumstances were, the debate is as old and commonplace as man; and it fell out with me, I suppose, as it falls with so many of my colleagues: I was found wanting in the strength to choose my better part, and embraced my worldly desires. It was not an easy consideration, for Father Whitechapel, as I have mentioned, was gaining sway over the banker; but the scales were finally tipped by that threat of removal from my post as Society treasurer, by which Bodkin's career would suffer smartingly, given Coutts's close ties to so many council members.

Yes, I preferred the complacent banker; and bade a farewell to the liberty, the comparative youth, the light step, pious compassion and near deification that I had enjoyed in the disguise of Father Whitechapel; although there was some unconscious reservation, for I neither gave up my hovel in the East End nor the drab outfits which still lay ready in my cabinet. So, too, I hastily made a lumping donation to the Society, in recompense for what I had previously commandeered (and which in fact was needed merely to keep the Society afloat)—and with this I thought the matter concluded.

IX

I resolved my future conduct to be nothing but the most proper and industrious; I convinced myself that even Father Whitechapel could not remedy London's ills, and that besides, the evils of the East End were its inhabitants' own doing. And I can say with honesty that my resolve turned fruitful. I laboured tirelessly at Coutts's in the beginning of the new year, and the happy result of these busy days was the partnership I had long awaited. But time began at last to obliterate the freshness of my alarm; my pangs of conscience began to grow into a thing of substance; the buried, yet insistent creature of Father Whitechapel whispered constantly at my ear; and at last, after a particularly pitiless bank meeting, whereby my advice on the marriage of two shipbuilding concerns led to dozens more unemployed, I once again compounded and swallowed the transforming draught.

I suppose, looking backward, that in my frenzied reunion with my estranged twin, I did not make enough allowance of the drug's diminishing efficacy—and it was by this that I was punished. Daily have I cursed myself for this foolishness; I can say only that at the time, foremost on my mind was Father Whitechapel's extreme virtue and humanity, from which it seemed that no evil could possibly arise. And indeed, my angel long caged, he came out soaring.

I was conscious, even when I took the draught, of a more unbridled and fervent desire to aid those unfortunates of the East End. It must have been this, I suppose, that led me to Clarke's Yard, frequented often by Rose Millett, that pitiful young woman that not long ago had slept beside Father Whitechapel. After a halting journey to that destination, I found her, battered and bloody after a turn with a brutish drunkard, and with an irrepressible sigh, I enfolded her and tended her wounds to the best of my abilities.

It was just as she had finally calmed that I felt the familiar sensations of transformation; yet the uninvited change came so sudden and swift that before I could flee or hide, the effects of the drug had worn off and I found myself in the shape of Geoffrey Bodkin, gasping and reeling, and looking straight at the petrified streetwalker. Yet despite the agonising danger at hand, I was not, at first, overly worried: even if she did recognise me, the woman, I reasoned, was no doubt familiar enough with gentlemen to know that I would pay and pay dearly for her silence. But within moments the prospect of such a solution was dashed to pieces. To my horror, the wench began wailing and shrieking, and made to run away. Instantly I grabbed her, feeling strong and rough, and, most lethal, raging to maintain silence at all cost. She felt like a plaything in my hands; and as she carried on screaming even with my hand clamped tight over her mouth, my love of life was stimulated; all vestiges of Father Whitechapel's mercy had vanished; even Bodkin's normal balancing instincts were stripped away. I thought of my career, my standing, my credit, and the damage this ungrateful strumpet might do with her noise and fuss; and a great flame of anger blazed up in me. Breaking out of all bounds, I clubbed my unhappy victim to the ground, pouncing atop her and mauling the throat of the unresisting body till I was certain she would never tell this tale.

Finally, weariness began to succeed, and in the top fit of my delirium, I was suddenly struck through the heart by a cold thrill of terror. A mist dispersed; I saw the lifeless body forfeited and fled from the scene, my fear of exposure screwed to the topmost peg. I ran to my room in the lodging house, where I hid my satchel and note-book; thence I set out through the squalid streets, hastening and hearkening in my wake for the steps of the law, even while light-headedly assuring myself that the trollop was, perhaps, better off dead than continuing in her living hell.

Even safely behind the bolted doors of my home and close to my drugs, the haze of panic still rent me from head to foot. I saw my life as a whole, followed it up from the days of childhood, when I had sat on my father's knee and learned to count coins, and through my own professional toils, to arrive again and again, with a sense of unreality, at the damned horrors of the evening. I could have screamed aloud at the tragic folly of it all: the murder of an innocent woman was appalling enough, but the crime would now draw abnormal attention from a city already up in arms by the Ripper murders and lusting for a suspect. I envisioned myself at the gallows if, indeed, a connexion were made between the murdered streetwalker and Bodkin; and the succeeding hours were spent in dumb shock and pure animal fear.

The night passed without incident, though, and as the acuteness of my fright began to die away, it was succeeded by a sense of liberation—for the problem of my conduct was solved. Father Whitechapel was thenceforth impossible: he may be a model of purity, but nevertheless, it was through him that Bodkin had fallen to unspeakable depravity; and now that the drug's power had been proven sorely unreliable, I was confined to the familiar part of my existence. And how I rejoiced to think it! With what willing surrender I embraced anew the restrictions of Bodkin's public life! With what sincere relief, I locked that laboratory door by which I had so often gone and come, and ground the key under my heel!

The next day, came the news that the murder had been overseen and the note-book recovered; this at first badly flustered me; yet as it were, the guilt of the crime fell squarely on Father Whitechapel; the name of Bodkin appeared safe. There were those who had met with the kindness of my second character and proclaimed his guilt impossible; but many others saw differently, and once the bounties came forth, all were on the lookout. As for myself, I think I was glad to know it; as staggering an injustice as it was for Father Whitechapel to be scapegoated as the Ripper, I was relieved to have my public life thus buttressed and guarded by the terrors of the scaffold. Bodkin was now my city of refuge; let that angel peep out but an instant, and the hands of all men would be raised to take him.

X

With Father Whitechapel shoved so resolutely—and, so I thought, permanently—into the abyss, I was true to my determination, leading a life of ferocious industry and enjoying the rich compensations of my approving employer. Nor can I say that I wholly chafed at this profitable and smug life; I think instead that I daily enjoyed it more completely, especially in light of my narrow escape from utter ruin. Yet still Bodkin was cursed with his old duality of purpose, and that merciful side of me, so long indulged and so recently chained back down, began to pray for licence.

I had been at a party at Meade's house till late at night, and once left alone with my old friend, my spiritual side a little drowsed from gin, and the animal within licking its chops, I was persuaded to visit Whitechapel (in the form of Bodkin) for a bout of undignified pleasure, as the two of us had done countless times in our youth. Even during the carriage ride to that district I began to feel a great anxiety, and once Meade and I went our separate ways on foot down Mile-End Road, the sight of that familiar street occasioned thoughts of the murdered young woman and the miserable lives of these bodies-for-hire. I could not bring myself to make that fleshly purchase; I sickened and froze at the mere thought; and going further, I pined to bring some solace to these streets, to atone for the low urges I had earlier thought to fulfil.

Not that I dreamed of resuscitating Father Whitechapel; the bare idea startled me into a frenzy. No, it was in my own person that I was once more tempted to quiet the assaults of my conscience and find penitence as a furtive almsgiver; therefore, in the shape of Bodkin, I bustled through Mile-End Road, emptying my pockets to all who begged at me.

I was not alarmed; the handouts seemed like a return to the old days before I discovered the drug—but it was this brief condescension to street-charity that instigated the final unbalancing of my soul. Suddenly a qualm came over me, a horrid nausea and the most deadly shuddering. These passed away, and left me faint; then as the faintness subsided, I was aware of a change in the temper of my thoughts, a greater piety, a love of humanity, a solution of the bonds of obligation. I looked down: my clothes hung formlessly on my narrowed limbs; the hand that lay on my knee was fair and bald. I was once more Father Whitechapel.

A moment before I had been wealthy, powerful, safe of all men's respect, the cloth laying for me in the dining-room at home. Now I was the quarry of mankind, London's foremost public enemy; a bounty on my head; thrall to the gallows— and set squarely in the neighbourhood where most readily recognised.

Bewildered at this drugless transformation, my reason wavered, but did not outright fail me. Left entirely to his own, Father Whitechapel would have most certainly succumbed to his sensibilities and remorse; he would have flown immediately to tend to the starving charges that might now consign him to the gallows. Yet somehow the residue of Bodkin's self-interest rose to the importance of the moment and mastered the complex. A strong dose of the drug might precipitate a return to my usual form—and by all grace there was still the dose stashed under the floorboards of my second home. But how was I to reach it? I was too well-known in the White-chapel lodging house, and I could not seek help from my servants; they would easily draw conclusions, let alone the danger of them henceforth connecting their master to Father Whitechapel. No, I saw I must employ another hand—and suddenly recalled Meade and the covered fly in the alleyway.

Thereupon, I arranged myself as best I could, and set forth on foot to Meade's cab, though this was a great and reckless gamble, being attired in misfitting clothes, an object marked out for observation, and amidst nocturnal stragglers that my passion raged like a tempest to embrace. Father Whitechapel felt no danger of his own life; he was too shaken with inordi-nate repentance at his creator's sins, too desperate for self-immolation; but he sped along to the designated alleyway, driven by Bodkin's fears, gliding through the less-frequented thoroughfares and watching for any hint of a police-officer. Once a woman spoke to him, offering, I think, a box of lights. He placed a pound-note in her hand and kissed her forehead; she clung to him, weeping, but he fled.

I was still somewhat doubtful whether Meade would abide such an intrusion and give credence to Bodkin's messenger, but I had underestimated how captivating my angel was to all who encountered him; for when Meade arrived back at the fly, I could not have wanted for a more obedient servant. And while Bodkin cared only for that metal box, Father White-chapel could hardly resist what he saw as his godly duty: putting before that sweater's sceptical eyes the helpless souls he exploited and that Father Whitechapel laboured to save. My intentions were good, but the terrible fate of Meade was most distressing to Bodkin; Father Whitechapel, too, reflected on the evening with regret, shedding tears for the broken manufacturer, whom he took (much like Bodkin) for a weak man controlled by base desires, though capable of salvation.

But soon enough Meade and his wakening were forgotten, for my present troubles were of an altogether different magnitude.

In the beginning, the difficulty had been to take a strong enough dose to throw off the body of Bodkin; next there was the problem of the drug's dwindling potency; but the recent change that had come over me on Mile-End Road was a menacing reversal of my previous experience. It appeared now that the drug itself was secondary, and the power of voluntary change waning. I began to spy the danger: the tide of blood had shifted; too long fettered, the saint that shared with me the phenomena of consciousness now seemed to be circumventing the need for the potion, presuming himself upon me with more unfamiliar and more awful pressure.

And as though my soul-mate showing me an example, after breakfasting the following morning and then stepping across the court to make my way to the bank, I was seized again with a premonitory shudder and had barely the time to gain the shelter of my cabinet before I was once again weeping with the passion of Father Whitechapel. It took on this occasion an enormous dose to recall me to myself; and alas! Scarcely were bankers' hours over that I was forced to flee home in a covered cab to re-administer the drug.

All things therefore seemed to point to this: I was losing hold of my original self, becoming incorporated with my second—and it would not be long before the balance of my nature was overturned permanently, and the character of Father Whitechapel became irrevocably mine.

XI

From that day forth I lived as though in a dream, a man eaten up and emptied by fever, languidly weak both in body and mind. At all hours of the day and night, I would be taken with those indescribable sensations that heralded the change; above all, if I slept, or even dozed for a moment in my chair, it was always as Father Whitechapel that I awakened. It was only under the immediate stimulation of the accursed draught, and that in alarmingly high doses, that I was able to wear the countenance of Bodkin; thus I was obliged to keep phials on my person at all times, such that I could continue at the bank.

When I slept, or when the virtue of the medicine wore off, I would leap almost without transition (for the pangs of transformation grew daily less marked) into the possession of a fancy brimming with images of unaided suffering, a soul boiling with repentance and writhing in the fires of abstinence—and yet with a body not quite strong enough to override Bodkin's raging instinct. And in those brief moments when Father Whitechapel lived, that disconsolate prisoner prostrated himself with infinite sadness of mien and streaming tears of sorrowful remorse, seeking to halt the millrace of hideous pictures swarming his memory, and praying to be paroled from his prison and sent forth to do his good deeds.

Still, despite this inner tumult, I did not hate Father Whitechapel. It was, for Bodkin, merely a thing of survival. He had seen the full character of that creature that was knit to him closer than an eye and was co-heir with him to death; and he thought of Father Whitechapel, for all his love of humanity, as something not only inorganic, but dangerously deranged. For given half a chance, the latter would have surrendered to his remorse and turned himself into the police, confessing to the murder in Clarke's Yard; indeed, he would have gladly endured retribution for the Ripper's entire spree of carnage, if that would save just one soul and calm the frightened city.

He, I say—it is sinful to say, I. That child of Heaven had nothing human; nothing lived in him but innocence and love; while in Bodkin, there now flamed only fear and hatred for those who would punish him. Bodkin stood shocked and even resentful at the creature's willingness to self-sacrifice—yet the feelings of Father Whitechapel for Bodkin were of a different order. Even as Bodkin prevailed against him and continually deposed him out of life, the angel still loved his master, as he loved all men; he felt no discontent for being regarded as a subordinate station of a part instead of a person; he, in fact, pitied Bodkin for the despondency in which the banker was now fallen. Hence the subtle signs he (Father Whitechapel) would send me, marking certain passages in my mother's Bible, and scrawling in my own hand cheques to various charities, even after Bodkin's bank account could no longer cover these donations and I was compelled to sate Father Whitechapel's charitable urges by giving away my fine furniture and beloved pictures.

Under the strain of this fearstruck existence and by sleeplessness beyond what I had thought possible to man, I became, in my own person of Geoffrey Bodkin, constantly under a crushing anticipation of disaster, white at the thought of surrendering control to the creature that slept within me, and solely occupied by one line of thought: the quantity of drugs remaining in my possession and the quickness by which I could obtain more. Yet as the great expense of these chemicals mounted, and as my capital was steadily depleted by donation cheques I did not even recall posting, I was driven in desperation to once again plunder the account of the Charity Society to the very hilt. And when that treasury became insufficient, I might have dared to pilfer from Coutts's itself—although that scheme was moot once it became impossible for me to continue at the bank; indeed, impossible for Geoffrey Bodkin to be in public.

XII

Eventually even tremendous doses of the draught were of scant efficacy: I could not wear the face of Geoffrey Bodkin for more than an hour or so. Further added to this misfortune was that I could no longer renew my dwindling provision of the salt and tincture. Indeed, Spencer ransacked London for any supplier willing to extend me further credit, but even the most capacious measure is emptied at last, and it was in vain—I was officially a bankrupt, fit for the workhouse. And while this indignity might have once froze Bodkin's blood, it now seemed a trifle compared to the much greater prospect of the gallows.

It is useless to prolong this description; let it suffice that no human has ever suffered so, and but for Father Whitechapel's abhorrence of the sin of self-destruction, I should have already released myself from these torments. Thinking now in retrospect, however, I am certain that it was largely (if not wholly) the preponderance of my second self that permitted me to bear the strain of impending doom. Bodkin in his love for life (or pure animal cowardice) surely would have been sent raving mad; yet Father Whitechapel, so careless of his own ego or gain, indeed his own corporeality, sat calmly in his lonely vigil, waiting for that heavy knock at the door.

In temptation of some miracle, I marshalled my remaining supply of the drug into one massive dose, which allowed me a day or two more before I (Bodkin) was severed permanently from my own face and nature. These last hours, however, were hardly happy ones, spent weeping in my chair, pacing up and down the cabinet, giving ear to every sound of menace. And quite as I expected, it was not long until Geoffrey Bodkin could no more think his own thoughts or see his own haggard face in the glass. He was now a prisoner in Father White-chapel's body, peering outward in fright, gaping and shuddering at my better half's acquiescence to arrest and mortal condemnation, and foretelling the chilling end of that grateful martyr.

XIII

There comes an end to all things; my three weeks are now exhausted. These shall be my last breaths of earthly air, and I can but pray for the mercy of God to send me to a better place. Whatever to come, though, concerns another than my-self; the remaining traces of Geoffrey Bodkin are so few and so dim, distant dots of light in a fog—but it is this trace amount that presses me to continue writing. Father White-chapel, that living prayer, has no interest in such self-regarding rambling; if left to his preference, this narrative would be cast aside and the Holy Book no more defaced; in-deed, his only yearning is to care for and comfort the other inmates, were he allowed leave of this dreary cage.

How dark these days! I wonder how it is that in sermons and tracts so little is said of the terrible suffering and weary black remorse that comes from infinite patience and humility, of the death of self and a life in God. And yet some have known it and found peace: those who wrote some of the saddest psalms knew it. But with London's wild absorption in Father Whitechapel's story, I cannot help thinking that this abject passion, this heartbreak that comes from living with the mind of Christ, would be not only strange, but unwelcome to others. There are so many difficulties to be faced, so many reproaches borne...

Ay, it seems unfathomable that a soul so pure shall trudge to the gallows, but in my heart I know my fate is deserved, for the sins so guiltily brought on by my original imperfect self. Forgive me, forgive me! Forgive me, Rose! Forgive me, Charles! Forgive me, London! How I have failed of what I hoped! How I have tottered and stumbled! How I have debased myself in the very brightness of an ideal!

But now! Time awfully fails me; the warders draw near, and I must lay down the pen and conclude this confession. Here then, with my final reckoning at hand, I put the reins in God's hands; I bow my head and say, "I am humble: give thy spirit to me; move me, guide me, be with me—I will bear. I seek only what is good."

About the Author

M. Elias Keller grew up in Bucks County, PA
and earned degrees in Anthropology and
Urban Studies from the University of
Pennsylvania. He has been a freelance and
journalistic writer in Philadelphia and San
Diego, as well as publishing short fiction in
various literary magazines. He lives in
Philadelphia.

www.MEliasKeller.com

READING GROUP GUIDE

1. In addition to a story about man's dual nature, *Strange Case of Dr. Jekyll & Mr. Hyde* has been read as an allegory of drug addiction, Victorian sexual repression, even homosexuality. What themes were most apparent to you while reading the story?

2. A common perception of the Jekyll & Hyde story is that Dr. Jekyll is good and Mr. Hyde is evil, but the story gains psychological complexity by the fact that Dr. Jekyll is both good *and* evil. Why do you think Stevenson wrote the story this way?

3. Why do you think the Jekyll and Hyde story is so often adapted? And now having read the original novel, did your opinion of the story change?

4. How do you view Mr. Bodkin and his guilt over being so rich while others are so poor? Do you think these feelings are common among the very wealthy?

5. Neither the Charity Organisation Society nor Father Whitechapel's methods seem to "cure" poverty. Do you prefer to contribute to an organization or give money directly to individual people? What would be your ideal form of charity?

6. *Strange Case of Mr. Bodkin & Father Whitechapel* implies that the Charity Organisation Society spends too much on overhead expenses and doesn't give enough to the poor. In recent years, there have been cases of financial mismanagement and gross inefficiencies at non-profit organizations, and foundations regularly spend large amounts on benefit dinners, salaries, and marketing and office expenses. What's your opinion of these practices, and do they change your view of charitable organizations?

7. Father Whitechapel dies as a martyr to Mr. Bodkin and the Ripper's sins, and also to the severe economic inequalities that created the deplorable conditions of London's East End in 19th century. Why do you think people who work to bring peace and equality to mankind often end up as martyrs?

Story of the Door

MR. UTTERSON THE LAWYER was a man of a rugged countenance that was never lighted by a smile; cold, scanty and embarrassed in discourse; backward in sentiment; lean, long, dusty, dreary and yet somehow lovable. At friendly meetings, and when the wine was to his taste, something eminently human beaconed from his eye; something indeed which never found its way into his talk, but which spoke not only in these silent symbols of the after-dinner face, but more often and loudly in the acts of his life. He was austere with himself; drank gin when he was alone, to mortify a taste for vintages; and though he enjoyed the theater, had not crossed the doors of one for twenty years. But he had an approved tolerance for others; sometimes wondering, almost with envy, at the high pressure of spirits involved in their misdeeds; and in any extremity inclined to help rather than to reprove. "I incline to Cain's heresy," he used to say quaintly: "I let my brother go to the devil in his own way." In this character, it was frequently his fortune to be the last reputable acquaintance and the last good influence in the lives of downgoing men. And to such as these, so long as they came about his chambers, he never marked a shade of change in his demeanour.

No doubt the feat was easy to Mr. Utterson; for he was undemonstrative at the best, and even his friendship seemed to be founded in a similar catholicity of good-nature. It is the mark of a modest man to accept his friendly circle ready-made from the hands of opportunity; and that was the lawyer's way. His friends were those of his own blood or those whom he had known the longest; his affections, like ivy, were the growth of time, they implied no aptness in the object. Hence, no doubt the bond that united him to Mr. Richard Enfield, his distant kinsman, the well-known man about town. It was a nut to crack for many, what these two could see in each other, or what subject they could find in common. It was reported by those who encountered them in their Sunday walks, that they said nothing, looked singularly dull and would hail with obvious relief the appearance of a friend. For all that, the two men put the greatest store by these excursions, counted them the chief jewel of each week, and not only set aside occasions of pleasure, but even resisted the calls of business, that they might enjoy them uninterrupted.

It chanced on one of these rambles that their way led them down a by-street in a busy quarter of London. The street was small and what is called quiet, but it drove a thriving trade on the weekdays. The inhabitants were all doing well, it seemed, and all emulously hoping to do better still, and laying out the surplus of their grains in coquetry; so that the shop fronts stood along that thoroughfare with an air of invitation, like rows of smiling saleswomen. Even on Sunday, when it veiled its more florid charms and lay comparatively empty of passage, the street shone out in contrast to its dingy neighbourhood, like a fire in a forest; and with its freshly painted shutters, well-polished brasses, and general cleanliness and gaiety of note, instantly caught and pleased the eye of the passenger.

Two doors from one corner, on the left hand going east the line was broken by the entry of a court; and just at that point a certain sinister block of building thrust forward its gable on the street. It was two storeys high; showed no window, nothing but a door on the lower storey and a blind forehead of discoloured wall on the upper; and bore in every feature, the marks of prolonged and sordid negligence. The door, which was equipped with neither bell nor knocker, was blistered and distained. Tramps slouched into the recess and struck matches on the panels; children kept shop upon the steps; the schoolboy had tried his knife on the mouldings; and for close on a generation, no one had appeared to drive away these random visitors or to repair their ravages.

Mr. Enfield and the lawyer were on the other side of the by-street; but when they came abreast of the entry, the former lifted up his cane and pointed.

"Did you ever remark that door?" he asked; and when his companion had replied in the affirmative: "It is connected in my mind," added he, "with a very odd story."

"Indeed?" said Mr. Utterson, with a slight change of voice, "and what was that?"

"Well, it was this way," returned Mr. Enfield: "I was coming home from some place at the end of the world, about three o'clock of a black winter morning, and my way lay through a part of town where there was literally nothing to be seen but lamps. Street after street and all the folks asleep— street after street, all lighted up as if for a procession and all as empty as a church— till at last I got into that state of mind when a man listens and listens and begins to long for the sight of a policeman. All at once, I saw two figures: one a little man who was stumping along eastward at a good walk, and the other a girl of maybe eight or ten who was running as hard as she was able down a cross street. Well, sir, the two ran into one another naturally enough at the corner; and then came the horrible part of the thing; for the man trampled calmly over the child's body and left her screaming on the ground. It sounds nothing to hear, but it was hellish to see. It wasn't like a man; it was like some damned Juggernaut. I gave a few halloa, took to my heels, collared my gentleman, and brought him back to where there was already quite a group about the screaming child. He was perfectly cool and made no resistance, but gave me one look, so ugly that it brought out the sweat on me like running. The people who had turned out were the girl's own family; and pretty soon, the doctor, for whom she had been sent put in his appearance. Well, the child was not much the worse, more frightened, according to the Sawbones; and there you might have supposed would be an end to it. But there was one curious circumstance. I had taken a loathing to my gentleman at first sight. So had the child's family, which was only natural. But the doctor's case was what struck me. He was the usual cut and dry apothecary, of no particular age and colour, with a strong Edinburgh accent and about as emotional as a bagpipe. Well, sir, he was like the rest of us; every time he looked at my prisoner, I saw that Sawbones turn sick and white with desire to kill him. I knew what was in his mind, just as he knew what was in mine; and killing being out of the question, we did the next best. We told the man we could and would make such a scandal out of this as should make his name stink from one end of London to the other. If he had any friends or any credit, we undertook that he should lose them. And all the time, as we were pitching it in red hot, we were keeping the women off him as best we could for they were as wild as harpies. I never saw a circle of such hateful faces; and there was the man in the middle, with a kind of black sneering coolness—frightened too, I could see that—but carrying it off, sir, really like Satan. 'If you choose to make capital out of this accident,' said he, 'I am naturally helpless. No gentleman but wishes to avoid a scene,' says he. 'Name your figure.' Well, we screwed him up to a hundred pounds for the child's family; he would have clearly liked to stick out; but there was something about the lot of us that meant mischief, and at last he struck. The next thing was to get the money; and where do you think he carried us but to that place with the door?—whipped out a key, went in, and presently came back with the matter of ten pounds in gold and a cheque for the balance on Coutts's, drawn payable to bearer and signed with a name that I can't mention, though it's one of the points of my story, but it was a name at least very well known and often printed. The figure was stiff; but the signature was good for more than that if it was only genuine. I took the liberty of pointing out to my gentleman that the whole business looked apocryphal, and that a man does not, in real life, walk into a cellar door at four in the morning and come out with another man's cheque for close upon a hundred pounds. But he was quite easy and sneering. 'Set your mind at rest,' says he, 'I will stay with you till the banks open and cash the cheque myself.' So we all set off, the doctor, and the child's father, and our friend and myself, and passed the rest of the night in my chambers; and next day, when we had breakfasted, went in a body to the bank. I gave in the cheque myself, and said I had every reason to believe it was a forgery. Not a bit of it. The cheque was genuine."

"Tut-tut," said Mr. Utterson.

"I see you feel as I do," said Mr. Enfield. "Yes, it's a bad story. For my man was a fellow that nobody could have to do with, a really damnable man; and the person that drew the cheque is the very pink of the proprieties, celebrated too, and (what makes it worse) one of your fellows who do what they call good. Black mail I suppose; an honest man paying through the nose for some of the capers of his youth. Black Mail House is what I call the place with the door, in consequence. Though even that, you know, is far from explaining all," he added, and with the words fell into a vein of musing.

From this he was recalled by Mr. Utterson asking rather suddenly: "And you don't know if the drawer of the cheque lives there?"

"A likely place, isn't it?" returned Mr. Enfield. "But I happen to have noticed his address; he lives in some square or other."

"And you never asked about the—place with the door?" said Mr. Utterson.

"No, sir: I had a delicacy," was the reply. "I feel very strongly about putting questions; it partakes too much of the style of the day of judgment. You start a question, and it's like starting a stone. You sit quietly on the top of a hill; and away the stone goes, starting others; and presently some bland old bird (the last you would have thought of) is knocked on the head in his own back garden and the family have to change their name. No sir, I make it a rule of mine: the more it looks like Queer Street, the less I ask."

"A very good rule, too," said the lawyer.

"But I have studied the place for myself," continued Mr. Enfield. "It seems scarcely a house. There is no other door, and nobody goes in or out of that one but, once in a great while, the gentleman of my adventure. There are three windows looking on the court on the first floor; none below; the windows are always shut but they're clean. And then there is a chimney which is generally smoking; so somebody must live there. And yet it's not so sure; for the buildings are so packed together about the court, that it's hard to say where one ends and another begins."

The pair walked on again for a while in silence; and then: "Enfield," said Mr. Utterson, "that's a good rule of yours."

"Yes, I think it is," returned Enfield.

"But for all that," continued the lawyer, "there's one point I want to ask: I want to ask the name of that man who walked over the child."

"Well," said Mr. Enfield, "I can't see what harm it would do. It was a man of the name of Hyde."

"Hm," said Mr. Utterson. "What sort of a man is he to see?"

"He is not easy to describe. There is something wrong with his appearance; something displeasing, something down-right detestable. I never saw a man I so disliked, and yet I scarce know why. He must be deformed somewhere; he gives a strong feeling of deformity, although I couldn't specify the point. He's an extraordinary looking man, and yet I really can name nothing out of the way. No, sir; I can make no hand of it; I can't describe him. And it's not want of memory; for I declare I can see him this moment."

Mr. Utterson again walked some way in silence and obviously under a weight of consideration. "You are sure he used a key?" he inquired at last.

"My dear sir..." began Enfield, surprised out of himself.

"Yes, I know," said Utterson; "I know it must seem strange. The fact is, if I do not ask you the name of the other party, it is because I know it already. You see, Richard, your tale has gone home. If you have been inexact in any point you had better correct it."

"I think you might have warned me," returned the other with a touch of sullenness. "But I have been pedantically exact, as you call it. The fellow had a key; and what's more, he has it still. I saw him use it not a week ago."

Mr. Utterson sighed deeply but said never a word; and the young man presently resumed. "Here is another lesson to say nothing," said he. "I am ashamed of my long tongue. Let us make a bargain never to refer to this again."

"With all my heart," said the lawyer. "I shake hands on that, Richard."

Search for Mr. Hyde

THAT EVENING MR. UTTERSON came home to his bachelor house in sombre spirits and sat down to dinner without relish. It was his custom of a Sunday, when this meal was over, to sit close by the fire, a volume of some dry divinity on his reading desk, until the clock of the neighbouring church rang out the hour of twelve, when he would go soberly and gratefully to bed. On this night however, as soon as the cloth was taken away, he took up a candle and went into his business room. There he opened his safe, took from the most private part of it a document endorsed on the envelope as Dr. Jekyll's Will and sat down with a clouded brow to study its contents. The will was holograph, for Mr. Utterson though he took charge of it now that it was made, had refused to lend the least assistance in the making of it; it provided not only that, in case of the decease of Henry Jekyll, M.D., D.C.L., L.L.D., F.R.S., etc., all his possessions were to pass into the hands of his "friend and benefactor Edward Hyde," but that in case of Dr. Jekyll's "disappearance or unexplained absence for any period exceeding three calendar months," the said Edward Hyde should step into the said Henry Jekyll's shoes without further delay and free from any burthen or obligation beyond the payment of a few small sums to the members of the doctor's household. This document had long been the lawyer's eyesore. It offended him both as a lawyer and as a lover of the sane and customary sides of life, to whom the fanciful was the immodest. And hitherto it was his ignorance of Mr. Hyde that had swelled his indignation; now, by a sudden turn, it was his knowledge. It was already bad enough when the name was but a name of which he could learn no more. It was worse when it began to be clothed upon with detestable attributes; and out of the shifting, insubstantial mists that had so long baffled his eye, there leaped up the sudden, definite presentment of a fiend.

"I thought it was madness," he said, as he replaced the obnoxious paper in the safe, "and now I begin to fear it is disgrace."

With that he blew out his candle, put on a greatcoat, and set forth in the direction of Cavendish Square, that citadel of medicine, where his friend, the great Dr. Lanyon, had his house and received his crowding patients. "If anyone knows, it will be Lanyon," he had thought.

The solemn butler knew and welcomed him; he was subjected to no stage of delay, but ushered direct from the door to the dining-room where Dr. Lanyon sat alone over his wine. This was a hearty, healthy, dapper, red-faced gentleman, with a shock of hair prematurely white, and a boisterous and decided manner. At sight of Mr. Utterson, he sprang up from his chair and welcomed him with both hands. The geniality, as was the way of the man, was somewhat theatrical to the eye; but it reposed on genuine feeling. For these two were old friends, old mates both at school and college, both thorough respecters of themselves and of each other, and what does not always follow, men who thoroughly enjoyed each other's company.

After a little rambling talk, the lawyer led up to the subject which so disagreeably preoccupied his mind.

"I suppose, Lanyon," said he, "you and I must be the two oldest friends that Henry Jekyll has?"

"I wish the friends were younger," chuckled Dr. Lanyon. "But I suppose we are. And what of that? I see little of him now."

"Indeed?" said Utterson. "I thought you had a bond of common interest."

"We had," was the reply. "But it is more than ten years since Henry Jekyll became too fanciful for me. He began to go wrong, wrong in mind; and though of course I continue to take an interest in him for old sake's sake, as they say, I see and I have seen devilish little of the man. Such unscientific balderdash," added the doctor, flushing suddenly purple, "would have estranged Damon and Pythias."

This little spirit of temper was somewhat of a relief to Mr. Utterson. "They have only differed on some point of science," he thought; and being a man of no scientific passions (except in the matter of conveyancing), he even added: "It is nothing worse than that!" He gave his friend a few seconds to recover his composure, and then approached the question he had come to put. "Did you ever come across a protégé of his—one Hyde?" he asked.

"Hyde?" repeated Lanyon. "No. Never heard of him. Since my time."

That was the amount of information that the lawyer carried back with him to the great, dark bed on which he tossed to and fro, until the small hours of the morning began to grow large. It was a night of little ease to his toiling mind, toiling in mere darkness and besieged by questions.

Six o'clock struck on the bells of the church that was so conveniently near to Mr. Utterson's dwelling, and still he was digging at the problem. Hitherto it had touched him on the intellectual side alone; but now his imagination also was engaged, or rather enslaved; and as he lay and tossed in the gross darkness of the night and the curtained room, Mr. Enfield's tale went by before his mind in a scroll of lighted pictures. He would be aware of the great field of lamps of a nocturnal city; then of the figure of a man walking swiftly; then of a child running from the doctor's; and then these met, and that human Juggernaut trod the child down and passed on regardless of her screams. Or else he would see a room in a rich house, where his friend lay asleep, dreaming and smiling at his dreams; and then the door of that room would be opened, the curtains of the bed plucked apart, the sleeper recalled, and lo! there would stand by his side a figure to whom power was given, and even at that dead hour, he must rise and do its bidding. The figure in these two phases haunted the lawyer all night; and if at any time he dozed over, it was but to see it glide more stealthily through sleeping houses, or move the more swiftly and still the more swiftly, even to dizziness, through wider labyrinths of lamplighted city, and at every street corner crush a child and leave her screaming. And still the figure had no face by which he might know it; even in his dreams, it had no face, or one that baffled him and melted before his eyes; and thus it was that there sprang up and grew apace in the lawyer's mind a singularly strong, almost an inordinate, curiosity to behold the features of the real Mr. Hyde. If he could but once set eyes on him, he thought the mystery would lighten and perhaps roll altogether away, as was the habit of mysterious things when well examined. He might see a reason for his friend's strange preference or bondage (call it which you please) and even for the startling clause of the will. At least it would be a face worth seeing: the face of a man who was without bowels of mercy: a face which had but to show itself to raise up, in the mind of the unimpressionable Enfield, a spirit of enduring hatred.

From that time forward, Mr. Utterson began to haunt the door in the by-street of shops. In the morning before office hours, at noon when business was plenty, and time scarce, at night under the face of the fogged city moon, by all lights and at all hours of solitude or concourse, the lawyer was to be found on his chosen post.

"If he be Mr. Hyde," he had thought, "I shall be Mr. Seek."

And at last his patience was rewarded. It was a fine dry night; frost in the air; the streets as clean as a ballroom floor; the lamps, unshaken by any wind, drawing a regular pattern of light and shadow. By ten o'clock, when the shops were closed, the by-street was very solitary and, in spite of the low growl of London from all round, very silent. Small sounds carried far; domestic sounds out of the houses were clearly audible on either side of the roadway; and the rumour of the approach of any passenger preceded him by a long time. Mr. Utterson had been some minutes at his post, when he was aware of an odd light footstep drawing near. In the course of his nightly patrols, he had long grown accustomed to the quaint effect with which the footfalls of a single person, while he is still a great way off, suddenly spring out distinct from the vast hum and clatter of the city. Yet his attention had never before been so sharply and decisively arrested; and it was with a strong, superstitious prevision of success that he withdrew into the entry of the court.

The steps drew swiftly nearer, and swelled out suddenly louder as they turned the end of the street. The lawyer, look-ing forth from the entry, could soon see what manner of man he had to deal with. He was small and very plainly dressed and the look of him, even at that distance, went somehow strongly against the watcher's inclination. But he made straight for the door, crossing the roadway to save time; and as he came, he drew a key from his pocket like one approaching home.

Mr. Utterson stepped out and touched him on the shoulder as he passed. "Mr. Hyde, I think?"

Mr. Hyde shrank back with a hissing intake of the breath. But his fear was only momentary; and though he did not look the lawyer in the face, he answered coolly enough: "That is my name. What do you want?"

"I see you are going in," returned the lawyer. "I am an old friend of Dr. Jekyll's—Mr. Utterson of Gaunt Street—you must have heard of my name; and meeting you so conveniently, I thought you might admit me."

"You will not find Dr. Jekyll; he is from home," replied Mr. Hyde, blowing in the key. And then suddenly, but still without looking up, "How did you know me?" he asked.

"On your side," said Mr. Utterson "will you do me a favour?"

"With pleasure," replied the other. "What shall it be?"

"Will you let me see your face?" asked the lawyer.

Mr. Hyde appeared to hesitate, and then, as if upon some sudden reflection, fronted about with an air of defiance; and the pair stared at each other pretty fixedly for a few seconds. "Now I shall know you again," said Mr. Utterson. "It may be useful."

"Yes," returned Mr. Hyde, "It is as well we have met; and à propos, you should have my address." And he gave a number of a street in Soho.

"Good God!" thought Mr. Utterson, "can he, too, have been thinking of the will?" But he kept his feelings to himself and only grunted in acknowledgment of the address.

"And now," said the other, "how did you know me?"

"By description," was the reply.

"Whose description?"

"We have common friends," said Mr. Utterson.

"Common friends," echoed Mr. Hyde, a little hoarsely. "Who are they?"

"Jekyll, for instance," said the lawyer.

"He never told you," cried Mr. Hyde, with a flush of anger. "I did not think you would have lied."

"Come," said Mr. Utterson, "that is not fitting language."

The other snarled aloud into a savage laugh; and the next moment, with extraordinary quickness, he had unlocked the door and disappeared into the house.

The lawyer stood awhile when Mr. Hyde had left him, the picture of disquietude. Then he began slowly to mount the street, pausing every step or two and putting his hand to his brow like a man in mental perplexity. The problem he was thus debating as he walked, was one of a class that is rarely solved. Mr. Hyde was pale and dwarfish, he gave an impression of deformity without any nameable malformation, he had a displeasing smile, he had borne himself to the lawyer with a sort of murderous mixture of timidity and boldness, and he spoke with a husky, whispering and somewhat broken voice; all these were points against him, but not all of these together could explain the hitherto unknown disgust, loathing and fear with which Mr. Utterson regarded him. "There must be something else," said the perplexed gentleman. "There is something more, if I could find a name for it. God bless me, the man seems hardly human! Something troglodytic, shall we say? or can it be the old story of Dr. Fell? or is it the mere radiance of a foul soul that thus transpires through, and transfigures, its clay continent? The last, I think; for, O my poor old Harry Jekyll, if ever I read Satan's signature upon a face, it is on that of your new friend."

Round the corner from the by-street, there was a square of ancient, handsome houses, now for the most part decayed from their high estate and let in flats and chambers to all sorts and conditions of men; map-engravers, architects, shady lawyers and the agents of obscure enterprises. One house, however, second from the corner, was still occupied entire; and at the door of this, which wore a great air of wealth and comfort, though it was now plunged in darkness except for the fanlight, Mr. Utterson stopped and knocked. A well-dressed, elderly servant opened the door.

"Is Dr. Jekyll at home, Poole?" asked the lawyer.

"I will see, Mr. Utterson," said Poole, admitting the visitor, as he spoke, into a large, low-roofed, comfortable hall paved with flags, warmed (after the fashion of a country house) by a bright, open fire, and furnished with costly cabinets of oak. "Will you wait here by the fire, sir? or shall I give you a light in the dining-room?"

"Here, thank you," said the lawyer, and he drew near and leaned on the tall fender. This hall, in which he was now left alone, was a pet fancy of his friend the doctor's; and Utterson himself was wont to speak of it as the pleasantest room in London. But tonight there was a shudder in his blood; the face of Hyde sat heavy on his memory; he felt (what was rare with him) a nausea and distaste of life; and in the gloom of his spirits, he seemed to read a menace in the flickering of the firelight on the polished cabinets and the uneasy starting of the shadow on the roof. He was ashamed of his relief, when

Poole presently returned to announce that Dr. Jekyll was gone out.

"I saw Mr. Hyde go in by the old dissecting room door, Poole," he said. "Is that right, when Dr. Jekyll is from home?"

"Quite right, Mr. Utterson, sir," replied the servant. "Mr. Hyde has a key."

"Your master seems to repose a great deal of trust in that young man, Poole," resumed the other musingly.

"Yes, sir, he does indeed," said Poole. "We have all orders to obey him."

"I do not think I ever met Mr. Hyde?" asked Utterson.

"O, dear no, sir. He never *dines* here," replied the butler. "Indeed we see very little of him on this side of the house; he mostly comes and goes by the laboratory."

"Well, good-night, Poole."

"Good-night, Mr. Utterson."

And the lawyer set out homeward with a very heavy heart. "Poor Harry Jekyll," he thought, "my mind misgives me he is in deep waters! He was wild when he was young; a long while ago to be sure; but in the law of God, there is no statute of limitations. Ay, it must be that; the ghost of some old sin, the cancer of some concealed disgrace: punishment coming, *pede claudo*, years after memory has forgotten and self-love condoned the fault." And the lawyer, scared by the thought, brooded awhile on his own past, groping in all the corners of memory, least by chance some Jack-in-the-Box of an old iniquity should leap to light there. His past was fairly blameless; few men could read the rolls of their life with less apprehension; yet he was humbled to the dust by the many ill things he had done, and raised up again into a sober and fearful gratitude by the many he had come so near to doing yet avoided.

And then by a return on his former subject, he conceived a spark of hope. "This Master Hyde, if he were studied," thought he, "must have secrets of his own; black secrets, by the look of him; secrets compared to which poor Jekyll's worst would be like sunshine. Things cannot continue as they are. It turns me cold to think of this creature stealing like a thief to Harry's bedside; poor Harry, what a wakening! And the danger of it; for if this Hyde suspects the existence of the will, he may grow impatient to inherit. Ay, I must put my shoulders to the wheel—if Jekyll will but let me," he added, "if Jekyll will only let me." For once more he saw before his mind's eye, as clear as transparency, the strange clauses of the will.

Dr. Jekyll Was Quite at Ease

A FORTNIGHT LATER, by excellent good fortune, the doctor gave one of his pleasant dinners to some five or six old cronies, all intelligent, reputable men and all judges of good wine; and Mr. Utterson so contrived that he remained behind after the others had departed. This was no new arrangement, but a thing that had befallen many scores of times. Where Utterson was liked, he was liked well. Hosts loved to detain the dry lawyer, when the light-hearted and loose-tongued had already their foot on the threshold; they liked to sit a while in his unobtrusive company, practising for solitude, sobering their minds in the man's rich silence after the expense and strain of gaiety. To this rule, Dr. Jekyll was no exception; and as he now sat on the opposite side of the fire—a large, well-made, smooth-faced man of fifty, with something of a stylish cast perhaps, but every mark of capacity and kindness—you could see by his looks that he cherished for Mr. Utterson a sincere and warm affection.

"I have been wanting to speak to you, Jekyll," began the latter. "You know that will of yours?"

A close observer might have gathered that the topic was distasteful; but the doctor carried it off gaily. "My poor Utterson," said he, "you are unfortunate in such a client. I never saw a man so distressed as you were by my will; unless it were that hide-bound pedant, Lanyon, at what he called my scientific heresies. O, I know he's a good fellow—you needn't frown—an excellent fellow, and I always mean to see more of him; but a hide-bound pedant for all that; an ignorant, blatant pedant. I was never more disappointed in any man than Lanyon."

"You know I never approved of it," pursued Utterson, ruthlessly disregarding the fresh topic.

"My will? Yes, certainly, I know that," said the doctor, a trifle sharply. "You have told me so."

"Well, I tell you so again," continued the lawyer. "I have been learning something of young Hyde."

The large handsome face of Dr. Jekyll grew pale to the very lips, and there came a blackness about his eyes. "I do not care to hear more," said he. "This is a matter I thought we had agreed to drop."

"What I heard was abominable," said Utterson.

"It can make no change. You do not understand my position," returned the doctor, with a certain incoherency of manner. "I am painfully situated, Utterson; my position is a very strange—a very strange one. It is one of those affairs that cannot be mended by talking."

"Jekyll," said Utterson, "you know me: I am a man to be trusted. Make a clean breast of this in confidence; and I make no doubt I can get you out of it."

"My good Utterson," said the doctor, "this is very good of you, this is downright good of you, and I cannot find words to thank you in. I believe you fully; I would trust you before any man alive, ay, before myself, if I could make the choice; but indeed it isn't what you fancy; it is not as bad as that; and just to put your good heart at rest, I will tell you one thing: the moment I choose, I can be rid of Mr. Hyde. I give you my hand upon that; and I thank you again and again; and I will just add one little word, Utterson, that I'm sure you'll take in good part: this is a private matter, and I beg of you to let it sleep."

Utterson reflected a little, looking in the fire.

"I have no doubt you are perfectly right," he said at last, getting to his feet.

"Well, but since we have touched upon this business, and for the last time I hope," continued the doctor, "there is one point I should like you to understand. I have really a very great interest in poor Hyde. I know you have seen him; he told me so; and I fear he was rude. But I do sincerely take a great, a very great interest in that young man; and if I am taken away, Utterson, I wish you to promise me that you will bear with him and get his rights for him. I think you would, if you knew all; and it would be a weight off my mind if you would promise."

"I can't pretend that I shall ever like him," said the lawyer.

"I don't ask that," pleaded Jekyll, laying his hand upon the other's arm; "I only ask for justice; I only ask you to help him for my sake, when I am no longer here."

Utterson heaved an irrepressible sigh. "Well," said he, "I promise."

The Carew Murder Case

NEARLY A YEAR LATER, in the month of October, 18—, London was startled by a crime of singular ferocity and rendered all the more notable by the high position of the victim. The details were few and startling. A maidservant living alone in a house not far from the river, had gone upstairs to bed about eleven. Although a fog rolled over the city in the small hours, the early part of the night was cloudless, and the lane, which the maid's window overlooked, was brilliantly lit by the full moon. It seems she was romantically given, for she sat down upon her box, which stood immediately under the window, and fell into a dream of musing. Never (she used to say, with streaming tears, when she narrated that experience), never had she felt more at peace with all men or thought more kindly of the world. And as she so sat she became aware of an aged beautiful gentleman with white hair, drawing near along the lane; and advancing to meet him, another and very small gentleman, to whom at first she paid less attention. When they had come within speech (which was just under the maid's eyes) the older man bowed and accosted the other with a very pretty manner of politeness. It did not seem as if the subject of his address were of great importance; indeed, from his pointing, it sometimes appeared as if he were only inquiring his way; but the moon shone on his face as he spoke, and the girl was pleased to watch it; it seemed to breathe such an innocent and old-world kindness of disposition, yet with something high too, as of a well-founded self-content. Presently her eye wandered to the other, and she was surprised to recognise in him a certain Mr. Hyde, who had once visited her master and for whom she had conceived a dislike. He had in his hand a heavy cane, with which he was trifling; but he answered never a word, and seemed to listen with an ill-contained impatience. And then all of a sudden he broke out in a great flame of anger, stamping with his foot, brandishing the cane, and carrying on (as the maid described it) like a madman. The old gentleman took a step back, with the air of one very much surprised and a trifle hurt; and at that Mr. Hyde broke out of all bounds and clubbed him to the earth. And next moment, with ape-like fury, he was trampling his victim under foot and hailing down a storm of blows, under which the bones were audibly shattered and the body jumped upon the roadway. At the horror of these sights and sounds, the maid fainted.

It was two o'clock when she came to herself and called for the police. The murderer was gone long ago; but there lay his victim in the middle of the lane, incredibly mangled. The stick with which the deed had been done, although it was of some rare and very tough and heavy wood, had broken in the middle under the stress of this insensate cruelty; and one splintered half had rolled in the neighbouring gutter—the other, without doubt, had been carried away by the murderer. A purse and gold watch were found upon the victim: but no cards or papers, except a sealed and stamped envelope, which he had been probably carrying to the post, and which bore the name and address of Mr. Utterson.

This was brought to the lawyer the next morning, before he was out of bed; and he had no sooner seen it and been told the circumstances, than he shot out a solemn lip. "I shall say nothing till I have seen the body," said he; "this may be very serious. Have the kindness to wait while I dress." And with the same grave countenance he hurried through his breakfast and drove to the police station, whither the body had been carried. As soon as he came into the cell, he nodded.

"Yes," said he, "I recognise him. I am sorry to say that this is Sir Danvers Carew."

"Good God, sir," exclaimed the officer, "is it possible?" And the next moment his eye lighted up with professional ambition. "This will make a deal of noise," he said. "And perhaps you can help us to the man." And he briefly narrated what the maid had seen, and showed the broken stick.

Mr. Utterson had already quailed at the name of Hyde; but when the stick was laid before him, he could doubt no longer; broken and battered as it was, he recognized it for one that he had himself presented many years before to Henry Jekyll.

"Is this Mr. Hyde a person of small stature?" he inquired.

"Particularly small and particularly wicked-looking, is what the maid calls him," said the officer.

Mr. Utterson reflected; and then, raising his head, "If you will come with me in my cab," he said, "I think I can take you to his house."

It was by this time about nine in the morning, and the first fog of the season. A great chocolate-coloured pall lowered over heaven, but the wind was continually charging and routing these embattled vapours; so that as the cab crawled from street to street, Mr. Utterson beheld a marvellous number of degrees and hues of twilight; for here it would be dark like the back-end of evening; and there would be a glow of a rich, lurid brown, like the light of some strange conflagration; and here, for a moment, the fog would be quite broken up, and a haggard shaft of daylight would glance in between the swirling wreaths. The dismal quarter of Soho seen under these changing glimpses, with its muddy ways, and slatternly passengers, and its lamps, which had never been extinguished or had been kindled afresh to combat this mournful reinvasion of darkness, seemed, in the lawyer's eyes, like a district of some city in a nightmare. The thoughts of his mind, besides, were of the gloomiest dye; and when he glanced at the companion of his drive, he was conscious of some touch of that terror of the law and the law's officers, which may at times assail the most honest.

As the cab drew up before the address indicated, the fog lifted a little and showed him a dingy street, a gin palace, a low French eating house, a shop for the retail of penny numbers and twopenny salads, many ragged children huddled in the doorways, and many women of many different nationalities passing out, key in hand, to have a morning glass; and the next moment the fog settled down again upon that part, as brown as umber, and cut him off from his blackguardly surroundings. This was the home of Henry Jekyll's favourite; of a man who was heir to a quarter of a million sterling.

An ivory-faced and silvery-haired old woman opened the door. She had an evil face, smoothed by hypocrisy: but her manners were excellent. Yes, she said, this was Mr. Hyde's, but he was not at home; he had been in that night very late, but he had gone away again in less than an hour; there was nothing strange in that; his habits were very irregular, and he was often absent; for instance, it was nearly two months since she had seen him till yesterday.

"Very well, then, we wish to see his rooms," said the lawyer; and when the woman began to declare it was impossible,

"I had better tell you who this person is," he added. "This is Inspector Newcomen of Scotland Yard."

A flash of odious joy appeared upon the woman's face. "Ah!" said she, "he is in trouble! What has he done?"

Mr. Utterson and the inspector exchanged glances. "He don't seem a very popular character," observed the latter. "And now, my good woman, just let me and this gentleman have a look about us."

In the whole extent of the house, which but for the old woman remained otherwise empty, Mr. Hyde had only used a couple of rooms; but these were furnished with luxury and good taste. A closet was filled with wine; the plate was of silver, the napery elegant; a good picture hung upon the walls, a gift (as Utterson supposed) from Henry Jekyll, who was much of a connoisseur; and the carpets were of many plies and agreeable in colour. At this moment, however, the rooms bore every mark of having been recently and hurriedly ransacked; clothes lay about the floor, with their pockets inside out; lock-fast drawers stood open; and on the hearth there lay a pile of grey ashes, as though many papers had been burned. From these embers the inspector disinterred the butt end of a green cheque book, which had resisted the action of the fire; the other half of the stick was found behind the door; and as this clinched his suspicions, the officer declared himself delighted. A visit to the bank, where several thousand pounds were found to be lying to the murderer's credit, completed his gratification.

"You may depend upon it, sir," he told Mr. Utterson: "I have him in my hand. He must have lost his head, or he never would have left the stick or, above all, burned the cheque book. Why, money's life to the man. We have nothing to do but wait for him at the bank, and get out the handbills."

This last, however, was not so easy of accomplishment; for Mr. Hyde had numbered few familiars—even the master of the servant maid had only seen him twice; his family could nowhere be traced; he had never been photographed; and the few who could describe him differed widely, as common observers will. Only on one point were they agreed; and that was the haunting sense of unexpressed deformity with which the fugitive impressed his beholders.

Incident of the Letter

I T WAS LATE IN THE AFTERNOON, when Mr. Utterson found his way to Dr. Jekyll's door, where he was at once admitted by Poole, and carried down by the kitchen offices and across a yard which had once been a garden, to the building which was indifferently known as the laboratory or dissecting rooms. The doctor had bought the house from the heirs of a celebrated surgeon; and his own tastes being rather chemical than anatomical, had changed the destination of the block at the bottom of the garden. It was the first time that the lawyer had been received in that part of his friend's quarters; and he eyed the dingy, windowless structure with curiosity, and gazed round with a distasteful sense of strangeness as he crossed the theatre, once crowded with eager students and now lying gaunt and silent, the tables laden with chemical apparatus, the floor strewn with crates and littered with packing straw, and the light falling dimly through the foggy cupola.

At the further end, a flight of stairs mounted to a door covered with red baize; and through this, Mr. Utterson was at last received into the doctor's cabinet. It was a large room fitted round with glass presses, furnished, among other things, with a cheval-glass and a business table, and looking out upon the court by three dusty windows barred with iron. The fire burned in the grate; a lamp was set lighted on the chimney shelf, for even in the houses the fog began to lie thickly; and there, close up to the warmth, sat Dr. Jekyll, looking deathly sick. He did not rise to meet his visitor, but held out a cold hand and bade him welcome in a changed voice.

"And now," said Mr. Utterson, as soon as Poole had left them, "you have heard the news?"

The doctor shuddered. "They were crying it in the square," he said. "I heard them in my dining-room."

"One word," said the lawyer. "Carew was my client, but so are you, and I want to know what I am doing. You have not been mad enough to hide this fellow?"

"Utterson, I swear to God," cried the doctor, "I swear to God I will never set eyes on him again. I bind my honour to you that I am done with him in this world. It is all at an end. And indeed he does not want my help; you do not know him as I do; he is safe, he is quite safe; mark my words, he will never more be heard of."

The lawyer listened gloomily; he did not like his friend's feverish manner. "You seem pretty sure of him," said he; "and for your sake, I hope you may be right. If it came to a trial, your name might appear."

"I am quite sure of him," replied Jekyll; "I have grounds for certainty that I cannot share with anyone. But there is one thing on which you may advise me. I have—I have received a letter; and I am at a loss whether I should show it to the police. I should like to leave it in your hands, Utterson; you would judge wisely, I am sure; I have so great a trust in you."

"You fear, I suppose, that it might lead to his detection?" asked the lawyer.

"No," said the other. "I cannot say that I care what becomes of Hyde; I am quite done with him. I was thinking of my own character, which this hateful business has rather exposed."

Utterson ruminated awhile; he was surprised at his friend's selfishness, and yet relieved by it. "Well," said he, at last, "let me see the letter."

The letter was written in an odd, upright hand and signed "Edward Hyde": and it signified, briefly enough, that the writer's benefactor, Dr. Jekyll, whom he had long so unworthily repaid for a thousand generosities, need labour under no alarm for his safety, as he had means of escape on which he placed a sure dependence. The lawyer liked this letter well enough; it put a better colour on the intimacy than he had looked for; and he blamed himself for some of his past suspicions.

"Have you the envelope?" he asked.

"I burned it," replied Jekyll, "before I thought what I was about. But it bore no postmark. The note was handed in."

"Shall I keep this and sleep upon it?" asked Utterson.

"I wish you to judge for me entirely," was the reply. "I have lost confidence in myself."

"Well, I shall consider," returned the lawyer. "And now one word more: it was Hyde who dictated the terms in your will about that disappearance?"

The doctor seemed seized with a qualm of faintness; he shut his mouth tight and nodded.

"I knew it," said Utterson. "He meant to murder you. You had a fine escape."

"I have had what is far more to the purpose," returned the doctor solemnly: "I have had a lesson—O God, Utterson, what a lesson I have had!" And he covered his face for a moment with his hands.

On his way out, the lawyer stopped and had a word or two with Poole. "By the bye," said he, "there was a letter handed in to-day: what was the messenger like?" But Poole was positive nothing had come except by post; "and only circulars by that," he added.

This news sent off the visitor with his fears renewed. Plainly the letter had come by the laboratory door; possibly, indeed, it had been written in the cabinet; and if that were so, it must be differently judged, and handled with the more caution. The newsboys, as he went, were crying themselves hoarse along the footways: "Special edition. Shocking murder of an M.P." That was the funeral oration of one friend and client; and he could not help a certain apprehension lest the good name of another should be sucked down in the eddy of the scandal. It was, at least, a ticklish decision that he had to make; and self-reliant as he was by habit, he began to cherish a longing for advice. It was not to be had directly; but perhaps, he thought, it might be fished for.

Presently after, he sat on one side of his own hearth, with Mr. Guest, his head clerk, upon the other, and midway between, at a nicely calculated distance from the fire, a bottle of a particular old wine that had long dwelt unsunned in the foundations of his house. The fog still slept on the wing above the drowned city, where the lamps glimmered like carbuncles; and through the muffle and smother of these fallen clouds, the procession of the town's life was still rolling in through the great arteries with a sound as of a mighty wind. But the room was gay with firelight. In the bottle the acids were long ago resolved; the imperial dye had softened with time, as the colour grows richer in stained windows; and the glow of hot autumn afternoons on hillside vineyards, was ready to be set free and to disperse the fogs of London. Insensibly the lawyer melted. There was no man from whom he kept fewer secrets than Mr. Guest; and he was not always sure that he kept as many as he meant. Guest had often been on business to the doctor's; he knew Poole; he could scarce have failed to hear of Mr. Hyde's familiarity about the house; he might draw conclusions: was it not as well, then, that he should see a letter which put that mystery to right? and above all since Guest, being a great student and critic of handwriting, would consider the step natural and obliging? The clerk, besides, was a man of counsel; he could scarce read so strange a document without dropping a remark; and by that remark Mr. Utterson might shape his future course.

"This is a sad business about Sir Danvers," he said.

"Yes, sir, indeed. It has elicited a great deal of public feeling," returned Guest. "The man, of course, was mad."

"I should like to hear your views on that," replied Utterson. "I have a document here in his handwriting; it is between ourselves, for I scarce know what to do about it; it is an ugly business at the best. But there it is; quite in your way: a murderer's autograph."

Guest's eyes brightened, and he sat down at once and studied it with passion. "No, sir," he said: "not mad; but it is an odd hand."

"And by all accounts a very odd writer," added the lawyer.

Just then the servant entered with a note.

"Is that from Dr. Jekyll, sir?" inquired the clerk. "I thought I knew the writing. Anything private, Mr. Utterson?"

"Only an invitation to dinner. Why? Do you want to see it?"

"One moment. I thank you, sir;" and the clerk laid the two sheets of paper alongside and sedulously compared their contents. "Thank you, sir," he said at last, returning both; "it's a very interesting autograph."

There was a pause, during which Mr. Utterson struggled with himself. "Why did you compare them, Guest?" he inquired suddenly.

"Well, sir," returned the clerk, "there's a rather singular resemblance; the two hands are in many points identical: only differently sloped."

"Rather quaint," said Utterson.

"It is, as you say, rather quaint," returned Guest.

"I wouldn't speak of this note, you know," said the master.

"No, sir," said the clerk. "I understand."

But no sooner was Mr. Utterson alone that night, than he locked the note into his safe, where it reposed from that time forward. "What!" he thought. "Henry Jekyll forge for a murderer!" And his blood ran cold in his veins.

Remarkable Incident of Dr. Lanyon

TIME RAN ON; thousands of pounds were offered in reward, for the death of Sir Danvers was resented as a public injury; but Mr. Hyde had disappeared out of the ken of the police as though he had never existed. Much of his past was unearthed, indeed, and all disreputable: tales came out of the man's cruelty, at once so callous and violent; of his vile life, of his strange associates, of the hatred that seemed to have surrounded his career; but of his present whereabouts, not a whisper. From the time he had left the house in Soho on the morning of the murder, he was simply blotted out; and gradually, as time drew on, Mr. Utterson began to recover from the hotness of his alarm, and to grow more at quiet with himself. The death of Sir Danvers was, to his way of thinking, more than paid for by the disappearance of Mr. Hyde. Now that that evil influence had been withdrawn, a new life began for Dr. Jekyll. He came out of his seclusion, renewed relations with his friends, became once more their familiar guest and entertainer; and whilst he had always been known for charities, he was now no less distinguished for religion. He was busy, he was much in the open air, he did good; his face seemed to open and brighten, as if with an inward consciousness of service; and for more than two months, the doctor was at peace.

On the 8th of January Utterson had dined at the doctor's with a small party; Lanyon had been there; and the face of the host had looked from one to the other as in the old days when the trio were inseparable friends. On the 12th, and again on the 14th, the door was shut against the lawyer. "The doctor was confined to the house," Poole said, "and saw no one." On the 15th, he tried again, and was again refused; and having now been used for the last two months to see his friend almost daily, he found this return of solitude to weigh upon his spirits. The fifth night he had in Guest to dine with him; and the sixth he betook himself to Dr. Lanyon's.

There at least he was not denied admittance; but when he came in, he was shocked at the change which had taken place in the doctor's appearance. He had his death-warrant written legibly upon his face. The rosy man had grown pale; his flesh had fallen away; he was visibly balder and older; and yet it was not so much these tokens of a swift physical decay that arrested the lawyer's notice, as a look in the eye and quality of manner that seemed to testify to some deep-seated terror of the mind. It was unlikely that the doctor should fear death; and yet that was what Utterson was tempted to suspect. "Yes," he thought; he is a doctor, he must know his own state and that his days are counted; and the knowledge is more than he can bear." And yet when Utterson remarked on his ill-looks, it was with an air of great firmness that Lanyon declared himself a doomed man.

"I have had a shock," he said, "and I shall never recover. It is a question of weeks. Well, life has been pleasant; I liked it; yes, sir, I used to like it. I sometimes think if we knew all, we should be more glad to get away."

"Jekyll is ill, too," observed Utterson. "Have you seen him?"

But Lanyon's face changed, and he held up a trembling hand. "I wish to see or hear no more of Dr. Jekyll," he said in a loud, unsteady voice. "I am quite done with that person; and I beg that you will spare me any allusion to one whom I regard as dead."

"Tut-tut," said Mr. Utterson; and then after a considerable pause, "Can't I do anything?" he inquired. "We are three very old friends, Lanyon; we shall not live to make others."

"Nothing can be done," returned Lanyon; "ask himself."

"He will not see me," said the lawyer.

"I am not surprised at that," was the reply. "Some day, Utterson, after I am dead, you may perhaps come to learn the right and wrong of this. I cannot tell you. And in the meantime, if you can sit and talk with me of other things, for God's sake, stay and do so; but if you cannot keep clear of this accursed topic, then in God's name, go, for I cannot bear it."

As soon as he got home, Utterson sat down and wrote to Jekyll, complaining of his exclusion from the house, and asking the cause of this unhappy break with Lanyon; and the next day brought him a long answer, often very pathetically worded, and sometimes darkly mysterious in drift. The quarrel with Lanyon was incurable. "I do not blame our old friend," Jekyll wrote, "but I share his view that we must never meet. I mean from henceforth to lead a life of extreme seclusion; you must not be surprised, nor must you doubt my friendship, if my door is often shut even to you. You must suffer me to go my own dark way. I have brought on myself a punishment and a danger that I cannot name. If I am the chief of sinners, I am the chief of sufferers also. I could not think that this earth contained a place for sufferings and terrors so unmanning; and you can do but one thing, Utterson, to lighten this destiny, and that is to respect my silence."

Utterson was amazed; the dark influence of Hyde had been withdrawn, the doctor had returned to his old tasks and amities; a week ago, the prospect had smiled with every promise of a cheerful and an honoured age; and now in a moment, friendship, and peace of mind, and the whole tenor of his life were wrecked. So great and unprepared a change pointed to madness; but in view of Lanyon's manner and words, there must lie for it some deeper ground.

A week afterwards Dr. Lanyon took to his bed, and in something less than a fortnight he was dead. The night after the funeral, at which he had been sadly affected, Utterson locked the door of his business room, and sitting there by the light of a melancholy candle, drew out and set before him an envelope addressed by the hand and sealed with the seal of his dead friend. "PRIVATE: for the hands of G. J. Utterson ALONE, and in case of his predecease *to be destroyed unread*," so it was emphatically superscribed; and the lawyer dreaded to behold the contents. "I have buried one friend to-day," he thought: "what if this should cost me another?" And then he condemned the fear as a disloyalty, and broke the seal. Within there was another enclosure, likewise sealed, and marked upon the cover as "not to be opened till the death or disappearance of Dr. Henry Jekyll." Utterson could not trust his eyes. Yes, it was disappearance; here again, as in the mad will which he had long ago restored to its author, here again were the idea of a disappearance and the name of Henry Jekyll bracketed. But in the will, that idea had sprung from the sinister suggestion of the man Hyde; it was set there with a purpose all too plain and horrible. Written by the hand of Lanyon, what should it mean? A great curiosity came on the trustee, to disregard the prohibition and dive at once to the bottom of these mysteries; but professional honour and faith to his dead friend were stringent obligations; and the packet slept in the inmost corner of his private safe.

It is one thing to mortify curiosity, another to conquer it; and it may be doubted if, from that day forth, Utterson desired the society of his surviving friend with the same eagerness. He thought of him kindly; but his thoughts were disquieted and fearful. He went to call indeed; but he was perhaps relieved to be denied admittance; perhaps, in his heart, he preferred to speak with Poole upon the doorstep and surrounded by the air and sounds of the open city, rather than to be admitted into that house of voluntary bondage, and to sit and speak with its inscrutable recluse.

Poole had, indeed, no very pleasant news to communicate. The doctor, it appeared, now more than ever confined himself to the cabinet over the laboratory, where he would sometimes even sleep; he was out of spirits, he had grown very silent, he did not read; it seemed as if he had something on his mind. Utterson became so used to the unvarying character of these reports, that he fell off little by little in the frequency of his visits.

Incident at the Window

I T CHANCED ON SUNDAY, when Mr. Utterson was on his usual walk with Mr. Enfield, that their way lay once again through the by-street; and that when they came in front of the door, both stopped to gaze on it.

"Well," said Enfield, "that story's at an end at least. We shall never see more of Mr. Hyde."

"I hope not," said Utterson. "Did I ever tell you that I once saw him, and shared your feeling of repulsion?"

"It was impossible to do the one without the other," returned Enfield. "And by the way, what an ass you must have thought me, not to know that this was a back way to Dr. Jekyll's! It was partly your own fault that I found it out, even when I did."

"So you found it out, did you?" said Utterson. "But if that be so, we may step into the court and take a look at the windows. To tell you the truth, I am uneasy about poor Jekyll; and even outside, I feel as if the presence of a friend might do him good."

The court was very cool and a little damp, and full of premature twilight, although the sky, high up overhead, was still bright with sunset. The middle one of the three windows was half-way open; and sitting close beside it, taking the air with an infinite sadness of mien, like some disconsolate prisoner, Utterson saw Dr. Jekyll.

"What! Jekyll!" he cried. "I trust you are better."

"I am very low, Utterson," replied the doctor drearily, "very low. It will not last long, thank God."

"You stay too much indoors," said the lawyer. "You should be out, whipping up the circulation like Mr. Enfield and me. (This is my cousin—Mr. Enfield—Dr. Jekyll.) Come now; get your hat and take a quick turn with us."

"You are very good," sighed the other. "I should like to very much; but no, no, no, it is quite impossible; I dare not. But indeed, Utterson, I am very glad to see you; this is really a great pleasure; I would ask you and Mr. Enfield up, but the place is really not fit."

"Why, then," said the lawyer, good-naturedly, "the best thing we can do is to stay down here and speak with you from where we are."

"That is just what I was about to venture to propose," returned the doctor with a smile. But the words were hardly uttered, before the smile was struck out of his face and succeeded by an expression of such abject terror and despair, as froze the very blood of the two gentlemen below. They saw it but for a glimpse for the window was instantly thrust down; but that glimpse had been sufficient, and they turned and left the court without a word. In silence, too, they traversed the by-street; and it was not until they had come into a neighbouring thoroughfare, where even upon a Sunday there were still some stirrings of life, that Mr. Utterson at last turned and looked at his companion. They were both pale; and there was an answering horror in their eyes.

"God forgive us, God forgive us," said Mr. Utterson.

But Mr. Enfield only nodded his head very seriously, and walked on once more in silence.

The Last Night

M R. UTTERSON WAS SITTING by his fireside one evening after dinner, when he was surprised to receive a visit from Poole.

"Bless me, Poole, what brings you here?" he cried; and then taking a second look at him, "What ails you?" he added; "is the doctor ill?"

"Mr. Utterson," said the man, "there is something wrong."

"Take a seat, and here is a glass of wine for you," said the lawyer. "Now, take your time, and tell me plainly what you want."

"You know the doctor's ways, sir," replied Poole, "and how he shuts himself up. Well, he's shut up again in the cabinet; and I don't like it, sir—I wish I may die if I like it. Mr. Utterson, sir, I'm afraid."

"Now, my good man," said the lawyer, "be explicit. What are you afraid of?"

"I've been afraid for about a week," returned Poole, doggedly disregarding the question, "and I can bear it no more."

The man's appearance amply bore out his words; his manner was altered for the worse; and except for the moment when he had first announced his terror, he had not once looked the lawyer in the face. Even now, he sat with the glass of wine untasted on his knee, and his eyes directed to a corner of the floor. "I can bear it no more," he repeated.

"Come," said the lawyer, "I see you have some good reason, Poole; I see there is something seriously amiss. Try to tell me what it is."

"I think there's been foul play," said Poole, hoarsely.

"Foul play!" cried the lawyer, a good deal frightened and rather inclined to be irritated in consequence. "What foul play! What does the man mean?"

"I daren't say, sir," was the answer; "but will you come along with me and see for yourself?"

Mr. Utterson's only answer was to rise and get his hat and greatcoat; but he observed with wonder the greatness of the relief that appeared upon the butler's face, and perhaps with no less, that the wine was still untasted when he set it down to follow.

It was a wild, cold, seasonable night of March, with a pale moon, lying on her back as though the wind had tilted her, and a flying wrack of the most diaphanous and lawny texture. The wind made talking difficult, and flecked the blood into the face. It seemed to have swept the streets unusually bare of passengers, besides; for Mr. Utterson thought he had never seen that part of London so deserted. He could have wished it otherwise; never in his life had he been conscious of so sharp a wish to see and touch his fellow-creatures; for struggle as he might, there was borne in upon his mind a crushing anticipation of calamity. The square, when they got there, was full of wind and dust, and the thin trees in the garden were lashing themselves along the railing. Poole, who had kept all the way a pace or two ahead, now pulled up in the middle of the pavement, and in spite of the biting weather, took off his hat and mopped his brow with a red pocket-handkerchief. But for all the hurry of his coming, these were not the dews of exertion that he wiped away, but the moisture of some strangling anguish; for his face was white and his voice, when he spoke, harsh and broken.

"Well, sir," he said, "here we are, and God grant there be nothing wrong."

"Amen, Poole," said the lawyer.

Thereupon the servant knocked in a very guarded manner; the door was opened on the chain; and a voice asked from within, "Is that you, Poole?"

"It's all right," said Poole. "Open the door."

The hall, when they entered it, was brightly lighted up; the fire was built high; and about the hearth the whole of the servants, men and women, stood huddled together like a flock of sheep. At the sight of Mr. Utterson, the housemaid broke into hysterical whimpering; and the cook, crying out "Bless God! it's Mr. Utterson," ran forward as if to take him in her arms.

"What, what? Are you all here?" said the lawyer peevishly. "Very irregular, very unseemly; your master would be far from pleased."

"They're all afraid," said Poole.

Blank silence followed, no one protesting; only the maid lifted her voice and now wept loudly.

"Hold your tongue!" Poole said to her, with a ferocity of accent that testified to his own jangled nerves; and indeed, when the girl had so suddenly raised the note of her lamentation, they had all started and turned towards the inner door with faces of dreadful expectation. "And now," continued the butler, addressing the knife-boy, "reach me a candle, and we'll get this through hands at once." And then he begged Mr. Utterson to follow him, and led the way to the back garden.

"Now, sir," said he, "you come as gently as you can. I want you to hear, and I don't want you to be heard. And see here, sir, if by any chance he was to ask you in, don't go."

Mr. Utterson's nerves, at this unlooked-for termination, gave a jerk that nearly threw him from his balance; but he recollected his courage and followed the butler into the laboratory building through the surgical theatre, with its lumber of crates and bottles, to the foot of the stair. Here Poole motioned him to stand on one side and listen; while he himself, setting down the candle and making a great and obvious call on his resolution, mounted the steps and knocked with a somewhat uncertain hand on the red baize of the cabinet door.

"Mr. Utterson, sir, asking to see you," he called; and even as he did so, once more violently signed to the lawyer to give ear.

A voice answered from within: "Tell him I cannot see anyone," it said complainingly.

"Thank you, sir," said Poole, with a note of something like triumph in his voice; and taking up his candle, he led Mr. Utterson back across the yard and into the great kitchen, where the fire was out and the beetles were leaping on the floor.

"Sir," he said, looking Mr. Utterson in the eyes, "Was that my master's voice?"

"It seems much changed," replied the lawyer, very pale, but giving look for look.

"Changed? Well, yes, I think so," said the butler. "Have I been twenty years in this man's house, to be deceived about his voice? No, sir; master's made away with; he was made away with eight days ago, when we heard him cry out upon the name of God; and *who's* in there instead of him, and why it stays there, is a thing that cries to Heaven, Mr. Utterson!"

"This is a very strange tale, Poole; this is rather a wild tale, my man," said Mr. Utterson, biting his finger. "Suppose it were as you suppose, supposing Dr. Jekyll to have been—well, murdered—what could induce the murderer to stay? That won't hold water; it doesn't commend itself to reason."

"Well, Mr. Utterson, you are a hard man to satisfy, but I'll do it yet," said Poole. "All this last week (you must know) him, or it, whatever it is that lives in that cabinet, has been crying night and day for some sort of medicine and cannot get it to his mind. It was sometimes his way—the master's, that is—to write his orders on a sheet of paper and throw it on the stair. We've had nothing else this week back; nothing but papers, and a closed door, and the very meals left there to be smuggled in when nobody was looking. Well, sir, every day, ay, and twice and thrice in the same day, there have been orders and complaints, and I have been sent flying to all the wholesale chemists in town. Every time I brought the stuff back, there would be another paper telling me to return it, because it was not pure, and another order to a different firm. This drug is wanted bitter bad, sir, whatever for."

"Have you any of these papers?" asked Mr. Utterson.

Poole felt in his pocket and handed out a crumpled note, which the lawyer, bending nearer to the candle, carefully examined. Its contents ran thus: "Dr. Jekyll presents his compliments to Messrs. Maw. He assures them that their last sample is impure and quite useless for his present purpose. In the year 18—, Dr. J. purchased a somewhat large quantity from Messrs. M. He now begs them to search with most sedulous care, and should any of the same quality be left, forward it to him at once. Expense is no consideration. The importance of this to Dr. J. can hardly be exaggerated." So far the letter had run composedly enough, but here with a sudden splutter of the pen, the writer's emotion had broken loose. "For God's sake," he added, "find me some of the old."

"This is a strange note," said Mr. Utterson; and then sharply, "How do you come to have it open?"

"The man at Maw's was main angry, sir, and he threw it back to me like so much dirt," returned Poole.

"This is unquestionably the doctor's hand, do you know?" resumed the lawyer.

"I thought it looked like it," said the servant rather sulkily; and then, with another voice, "But what matters hand of write?" he said. "I've seen him!"

"Seen him?" repeated Mr. Utterson. "Well?"

"That's it!" said Poole. "It was this way. I came suddenly into the theatre from the garden. It seems he had slipped out to look for this drug or whatever it is; for the cabinet door was open, and there he was at the far end of the room digging among the crates. He looked up when I came in, gave a kind of cry, and whipped upstairs into the cabinet. It was but for one minute that I saw him, but the hair stood upon my head like quills. Sir, if that was my master, why had he a mask upon his face? If it was my master, why did he cry out like a rat, and run from me? I have served him long enough. And then..." The man paused and passed his hand over his face.

"These are all very strange circumstances," said Mr. Utterson, "but I think I begin to see daylight. Your master, Poole, is plainly seized with one of those maladies that both torture and deform the sufferer; hence, for aught I know, the alteration of his voice; hence the mask and the avoidance of his friends; hence his eagerness to find this drug, by means of which the poor soul retains some hope of ultimate recovery—

God grant that he be not deceived! There is my explanation; it is sad enough, Poole, ay, and appalling to consider; but it is plain and natural, hangs well together, and delivers us from all exorbitant alarms."

"Sir," said the butler, turning to a sort of mottled pallor, "that thing was not my master, and there's the truth. My master"—here he looked round him and began to whisper—"is a tall, fine build of a man, and this was more of a dwarf." Utterson attempted to protest. "O, sir," cried Poole, "do you think I do not know my master after twenty years? Do you think I do not know where his head comes to in the cabinet door, where I saw him every morning of my life? No, sir, that thing in the mask was never Dr. Jekyll—God knows what it was, but it was never Dr. Jekyll; and it is the belief of my heart that there was murder done."

"Poole," replied the lawyer, "if you say that, it will become my duty to make certain. Much as I desire to spare your master's feelings, much as I am puzzled by this note which seems to prove him to be still alive, I shall consider it my duty to break in that door."

"Ah, Mr. Utterson, that's talking!" cried the butler.

"And now comes the second question," resumed Utterson: "Who is going to do it?"

"Why, you and me, sir," was the undaunted reply.

"That's very well said," returned the lawyer; "and whatever comes of it, I shall make it my business to see you are no loser."

"There is an axe in the theatre," continued Poole; "and you might take the kitchen poker for yourself."

The lawyer took that rude but weighty instrument into his hand, and balanced it. "Do you know, Poole," he said, looking up, "that you and I are about to place ourselves in a position of some peril?"

"You may say so, sir, indeed," returned the butler.

"It is well, then that we should be frank," said the other. "We both think more than we have said; let us make a clean breast. This masked figure that you saw, did you recognise it?"

"Well, sir, it went so quick, and the creature was so doubled up, that I could hardly swear to that," was the answer. "But if you mean, was it Mr. Hyde?—why, yes, I think it was!" You see, it was much of the same bigness; and it had the same quick, light way with it; and then who else could have got in by the laboratory door? You have not forgot, sir, that at the time of the murder he had still the key with him? But that's not all. I don't know, Mr. Utterson, if you ever met this Mr. Hyde?"

"Yes," said the lawyer, "I once spoke with him."

"Then you must know as well as the rest of us that there was something queer about that gentleman—something that gave a man a turn—I don't know rightly how to say it, sir, beyond this: that you felt in your marrow kind of cold and thin."

"I own I felt something of what you describe," said Mr. Utterson.

"Quite so, sir," returned Poole. "Well, when that masked thing like a monkey jumped from among the chemicals and whipped into the cabinet, it went down my spine like ice. O, I know it's not evidence, Mr. Utterson; I'm book-learned enough for that; but a man has his feelings, and I give you my bible-word it was Mr. Hyde!"

"Ay, ay," said the lawyer. "My fears incline to the same point. Evil, I fear, founded—evil was sure to come—of that connection. Ay truly, I believe you; I believe poor Harry is killed; and I believe his murderer (for what purpose, God alone can tell) is still lurking in his victim's room. Well, let our name be vengeance. Call Bradshaw."

The footman came at the summons, very white and nervous.

"Put yourself together, Bradshaw," said the lawyer. "This suspense, I know, is telling upon all of you; but it is now our intention to make an end of it. Poole, here, and I are going to force our way into the cabinet. If all is well, my shoulders are broad enough to bear the blame. Meanwhile, lest anything should really be amiss, or any malefactor seek to escape by the back, you and the boy must go round the corner with a pair of good sticks and take your post at the laboratory door. We give you ten minutes, to get to your stations."

As Bradshaw left, the lawyer looked at his watch. "And now, Poole, let us get to ours," he said; and taking the poker under his arm, led the way into the yard. The scud had banked over the moon, and it was now quite dark. The wind, which only broke in puffs and draughts into that deep well of building, tossed the light of the candle to and fro about their steps, until they came into the shelter of the theatre, where they sat down silently to wait. London hummed solemnly all around; but nearer at hand, the stillness was only broken by the sounds of a footfall moving to and fro along the cabinet floor.

"So it will walk all day, sir," whispered Poole; "ay, and the better part of the night. Only when a new sample comes from the chemist, there's a bit of a break. Ah, it's an ill conscience that's such an enemy to rest! Ah, sir, there's blood foully shed in every step of it! But hark again, a little closer—put your heart in your ears, Mr. Utterson, and tell me, is that the doctor's foot?"

The steps fell lightly and oddly, with a certain swing, for all they went so slowly; it was different indeed from the heavy creaking tread of Henry Jekyll. Utterson sighed. "Is there never anything else?" he asked.

Poole nodded. "Once," he said. "Once I heard it weeping!"

"Weeping? how that?" said the lawyer, conscious of a sudden chill of horror.

"Weeping like a woman or a lost soul," said the butler. "I came away with that upon my heart, that I could have wept too."

But now the ten minutes drew to an end. Poole disinterred the axe from under a stack of packing straw; the candle was set upon the nearest table to light them to the attack; and they drew near with bated breath to where that patient foot was still going up and down, up and down, in the quiet of the night. "Jekyll," cried Utterson, with a loud voice, "I demand to see you." He paused a moment, but there came no reply. "I give you fair warning, our suspicions are aroused, and I must and shall see you," he resumed; "if not by fair means, then by foul—if not of your consent, then by brute force!"

"Utterson," said the voice, "for God's sake, have mercy!"

"Ah, that's not Jekyll's voice—it's Hyde's!" cried Utterson. "Down with the door, Poole!"

Poole swung the axe over his shoulder; the blow shook the building, and the red baize door leaped against the lock and hinges. A dismal screech, as of mere animal terror, rang from the cabinet. Up went the axe again, and again the panels crashed and the frame bounded; four times the blow fell; but the wood was tough and the fittings were of excellent workmanship; and it was not until the fifth, that the lock burst and the wreck of the door fell inwards on the carpet.

The besiegers, appalled by their own riot and the stillness that had succeeded, stood back a little and peered in. There lay the cabinet before their eyes in the quiet lamplight, a good fire glowing and chattering on the hearth, the kettle singing its thin strain, a drawer or two open, papers neatly set forth on the business table, and nearer the fire, the things laid out for tea; the quietest room, you would have said, and, but for the glazed presses full of chemicals, the most commonplace that night in London.

Right in the middle there lay the body of a man sorely contorted and still twitching. They drew near on tiptoe, turned it on its back and beheld the face of Edward Hyde. He was dressed in clothes far too large for him, clothes of the doctor's bigness; the cords of his face still moved with a semblance of life, but life was quite gone: and by the crushed phial in the hand and the strong smell of kernels that hung upon the air, Utterson knew that he was looking on the body of a self-destroyer.

"We have come too late," he said sternly, "whether to save or punish. Hyde is gone to his account; and it only remains for us to find the body of your master."

The far greater proportion of the building was occupied by the theatre, which filled almost the whole ground storey and was lighted from above, and by the cabinet, which formed an upper story at one end and looked upon the court. A corridor joined the theatre to the door on the by-street; and with this the cabinet communicated separately by a second flight of stairs. There were besides a few dark closets and a spacious cellar. All these they now thoroughly examined. Each closet needed but a glance, for all were empty, and all, by the dust that fell from their doors, had stood long unopened. The cellar, indeed, was filled with crazy lumber, mostly dating from the times of the surgeon who was Jekyll's predecessor; but even as they opened the door they were advertised of the uselessness of further search, by the fall of a perfect mat of cobweb which had for years sealed up the entrance. Nowhere was there any trace of Henry Jekyll, dead or alive.

Poole stamped on the flags of the corridor. "He must be buried here," he said, hearkening to the sound.

"Or he may have fled," said Utterson, and he turned to examine the door in the by-street. It was locked; and lying nearby on the flags, they found the key, already stained with rust.

"This does not look like use," observed the lawyer.

"Use!" echoed Poole. "Do you not see, sir, it is broken? much as if a man had stamped on it."

"Ay," continued Utterson, "and the fractures, too, are rusty." The two men looked at each other with a scare. "This is beyond me, Poole," said the lawyer. "Let us go back to the cabinet."

They mounted the stair in silence, and still with an occasional awestruck glance at the dead body, proceeded more thoroughly to examine the contents of the cabinet. At one table, there were traces of chemical work, various measured heaps of some white salt being laid on glass saucers, as though for an experiment in which the unhappy man had been prevented.

"That is the same drug that I was always bringing him," said Poole; and even as he spoke, the kettle with a startling noise boiled over.

This brought them to the fireside, where the easy-chair was drawn cosily up, and the tea things stood ready to the sitter's elbow, the very sugar in the cup. There were several books on a shelf; one lay beside the tea things open, and Utterson was amazed to find it a copy of a pious work, for which Jekyll had several times expressed a great esteem, annotated, in his own hand with startling blasphemies.

Next, in the course of their review of the chamber, the searchers came to the cheval-glass, into whose depths they looked with an involuntary horror. But it was so turned as to show them nothing but the rosy glow playing on the roof, the fire sparkling in a hundred repetitions along the glazed front of the presses, and their own pale and fearful countenances stooping to look in.

"This glass has seen some strange things, sir," whispered Poole.

"And surely none stranger than itself," echoed the lawyer in the same tones. "For what did Jekyll"—he caught himself up at the word with a start, and then conquering the weakness—"what could Jekyll want with it?" he said.

"You may say that!" said Poole.

Next they turned to the business table. On the desk, among the neat array of papers, a large envelope was uppermost, and bore, in the doctor's hand, the name of Mr. Utterson. The lawyer unsealed it, and several enclosures fell to the floor. The first was a will, drawn in the same eccentric terms as the one which he had returned six months before, to serve as a testament in case of death and as a deed of gift in case of disappearance; but in place of the name of Edward Hyde, the lawyer, with indescribable amazement read the name of Gabriel John Utterson. He looked at Poole, and then back at the paper, and last of all at the dead malefactor stretched upon the carpet.

"My head goes round," he said. "He has been all these days in possession; he had no cause to like me; he must have raged to see himself displaced; and he has not destroyed this document."

He caught up the next paper; it was a brief note in the doctor's hand and dated at the top. "O Poole!" the lawyer cried, "he was alive and here this day. He cannot have been disposed of in so short a space; he must be still alive, he must have fled! And then, why fled? and how? and in that case, can we venture to declare this suicide? O, we must be careful. I foresee that we may yet involve your master in some dire catastrophe."

"Why don't you read it, sir?" asked Poole.

"Because I fear," replied the lawyer solemnly. "God grant I have no cause for it!" And with that he brought the paper to his eyes and read as follows:

"My dear Utterson,—When this shall fall into your hands, I shall have disappeared, under what circumstances I have not the penetration to foresee, but my instinct and all the circumstances of my nameless situation tell me that the end is sure and must be early. Go then, and first read the narrative which Lanyon warned me he was to place in your hands; and if you care to hear more, turn to the confession of

"Your unworthy and unhappy friend,
"HENRY JEKYLL."

"There was a third enclosure?" asked Utterson.

"Here, sir," said Poole, and gave into his hands a considerable packet sealed in several places.

The lawyer put it in his pocket. "I would say nothing of this paper. If your master has fled or is dead, we may at least save his credit. It is now ten; I must go home and read these documents in quiet; but I shall be back before midnight, when we shall send for the police."

They went out, locking the door of the theatre behind them; and Utterson, once more leaving the servants gathered about the fire in the hall, trudged back to his office to read the two narratives in which this mystery was now to be explained.

Dr. Lanyon's Narrative

O N THE NINTH OF JANUARY, now four days ago, I received by the evening delivery a registered envelope, addressed in the hand of my colleague and old school companion, Henry Jekyll. I was a good deal surprised by this; for we were by no means in the habit of correspondence; I had seen the man, dined with him, indeed, the night before; and I could imagine nothing in our intercourse that should justify formality of registration. The contents increased my wonder; for this is how the letter ran:

"10th December, 18—.
"Dear Lanyon,—You are one of my oldest friends; and although we may have differed at times on scientific questions, I cannot remember, at least on my side, any break in our affection. There was never a day when, if you had said to me, 'Jekyll, my life, my honour, my reason, depend upon you,' I would not have sacrificed my left hand to help you. Lanyon my life, my honour, my reason, are all at your mercy; if you fail me to-night, I am lost. You might suppose, after this preface, that I am going to ask you for something dishonourable to grant. Judge for yourself.

"I want you to postpone all other engagements for to-night—ay, even if you were summoned to the bedside

of an emperor; to take a cab, unless your carriage should
be actually at the door; and with this letter in your hand
for consultation, to drive straight to my house. Poole,
my butler, has his orders; you will find him waiting your
arrival with a locksmith. The door of my cabinet is then
to be forced: and you are to go in alone; to open the
glazed press (letter E) on the left hand, breaking the
lock if it be shut; and to draw out, *with all its contents as
they stand*, the fourth drawer from the top or (which is
the same thing) the third from the bottom. In my extreme distress of mind, I have a morbid fear of
misdirecting you; but even if I am in error, you may
know the right drawer by its contents: some powders, a
phial and a paper book. This drawer I beg of you to carry back with you to Cavendish Square exactly as it
stands.

"That is the first part of the service: now for the second. You should be back, if you set out at once on the
receipt of this, long before midnight; but I will leave
you that amount of margin, not only in the fear of one
of those obstacles that can neither be prevented nor
foreseen, but because an hour when your servants are in
bed is to be preferred for what will then remain to do.
At midnight, then, I have to ask you to be alone in your
consulting room, to admit with your own hand into the
house a man who will present himself in my name, and
to place in his hands the drawer that you will have
brought with you from my cabinet. Then you will have
played your part and earned my gratitude completely.
Five minutes afterwards, if you insist upon an explanation, you will have understood that these arrangements
are of capital importance; and that by the neglect of one

of them, fantastic as they must appear, you might have charged your conscience with my death or the shipwreck of my reason.

"Confident as I am that you will not trifle with this appeal, my heart sinks and my hand trembles at the bare thought of such a possibility. Think of me at this hour, in a strange place, labouring under a blackness of distress that no fancy can exaggerate, and yet well aware that, if you will but punctually serve me, my troubles will roll away like a story that is told. Serve me, my dear Lanyon and save

"Your friend, "H.J.

"P.S.—I had already sealed this up when a fresh terror struck upon my soul. It is possible that the post-office may fail me, and this letter not come into your hands until to-morrow morning. In that case, dear Lanyon, do my errand when it shall be most convenient for you in the course of the day; and once more expect my messenger at midnight. It may then already be too late; and if that night passes without event, you will know that you have seen the last of Henry Jekyll."

Upon the reading of this letter, I made sure my colleague was insane; but till that was proved beyond the possibility of doubt, I felt bound to do as he requested. The less I understood of this farrago, the less I was in a position to judge of its importance; and an appeal so worded could not be set aside without a grave responsibility. I rose accordingly from table, got into a hansom, and drove straight to Jekyll's house. The butler was awaiting my arrival; he had received by the same post as mine a registered letter of instruction, and had sent at once for a locksmith and a carpenter. The tradesmen came while we were yet speaking; and we moved in a body to old Dr. Denman's surgical theatre, from which (as you are doubtless aware) Jekyll's private cabinet is most conveniently entered. The door was very strong, the lock excellent; the carpenter avowed he would have great trouble and have to do much damage, if force were to be used; and the locksmith was near despair. But this last was a handy fellow, and after two hour's work, the door stood open. The press marked E was unlocked; and I took out the drawer, had it filled up with straw and tied in a sheet, and returned with it to Cavendish Square.

Here I proceeded to examine its contents. The powders were neatly enough made up, but not with the nicety of the dispensing chemist; so that it was plain they were of Jekyll's private manufacture: and when I opened one of the wrappers I found what seemed to me a simple crystalline salt of a white colour. The phial, to which I next turned my attention, might have been about half full of a blood-red liquor, which was highly pungent to the sense of smell and seemed to me to contain phosphorus and some volatile ether. At the other ingredients I could make no guess. The book was an ordinary version book and contained little but a series of dates. These covered a period of many years, but I observed that the entries ceased nearly a year ago and quite abruptly. Here and there a brief remark was appended to a date, usually no more than a single word: "double" occurring perhaps six times in a total of several hundred entries; and once very early in the list and followed by several marks of exclamation, "total failure!!!" All this, though it whetted my curiosity, told me little that was definite. Here were a phial of some tincture, a paper of some salt, and the record of a series of experiments that had led (like too many of Jekyll's investigations) to no end of practical usefulness. How could the presence of these articles in my house affect either the honour, the sanity, or the life of my flighty colleague? If his messenger could go to one place, why could he not go to another? And even granting some impediment, why was this gentleman to be received by me in secret? The more I reflected the more convinced I grew that I was dealing with a case of cerebral disease; and though I dismissed my servants to bed, I loaded an old revolver, that I might be found in some posture of self-defence.

Twelve o'clock had scarce rung out over London, ere the knocker sounded very gently on the door. I went myself at the summons, and found a small man crouching against the pillars of the portico.

"Are you come from Dr. Jekyll?" I asked.

He told me "yes" by a constrained gesture; and when I had bidden him enter, he did not obey me without a searching backward glance into the darkness of the square. There was a policeman not far off, advancing with his bull's eye open; and at the sight, I thought my visitor started and made greater haste.

These particulars struck me, I confess, disagreeably; and as I followed him into the bright light of the consulting room, I kept my hand ready on my weapon. Here, at last, I had a chance of clearly seeing him. I had never set eyes on him before, so much was certain. He was small, as I have said; I was struck besides with the shocking expression of his face, with his remarkable combination of great muscular activity and great apparent debility of constitution, and—last but not least—with the odd, subjective disturbance caused by his neighbourhood. This bore some resemblance to incipient rigour, and was accompanied by a marked sinking of the pulse. At the time, I set it down to some idiosyncratic, personal distaste, and merely wondered at the acuteness of the symptoms; but I have since had reason to believe the cause to lie much deeper in the nature of man, and to turn on some nobler hinge than the principle of hatred.

This person (who had thus, from the first moment of his entrance, struck in me what I can only, describe as a disgustful curiosity) was dressed in a fashion that would have made an ordinary person laughable; his clothes, that is to say, although they were of rich and sober fabric, were enormously too large for him in every measurement—the trousers hanging on his legs and rolled up to keep them from the ground, the waist of the coat below his haunches, and the collar sprawling wide upon his shoulders. Strange to relate, this ludicrous accoutrement was far from moving me to laughter. Rather, as there was something abnormal and misbegotten in the very essence of the creature that now faced me—something seizing, surprising and revolting—this fresh disparity seemed but to fit in with and to reinforce it; so that to my interest in the man's nature and character, there was added a curiosity as to his origin, his life, his fortune and status in the world.

These observations, though they have taken so great a space to be set down in, were yet the work of a few seconds. My visitor was, indeed, on fire with sombre excitement.

"Have you got it?" he cried. "Have you got it?" And so lively was his impatience that he even laid his hand upon my arm and sought to shake me.

I put him back, conscious at his touch of a certain icy pang along my blood. "Come, sir," said I. "You forget that I have not yet the pleasure of your acquaintance. Be seated, if you please." And I showed him an example, and sat down myself in my customary seat and with as fair an imitation of my ordinary manner to a patient, as the lateness of the hour, the nature of my preoccupations, and the horror I had of my visitor, would suffer me to muster.

"I beg your pardon, Dr. Lanyon," he replied civilly enough. "What you say is very well founded; and my impatience has shown its heels to my politeness. I come here at the instance of your colleague, Dr. Henry Jekyll, on a piece of business of some moment; and I understood..." He paused and put his hand to his throat, and I could see, in spite of his collected manner, that he was wrestling against the approaches of the hysteria—"I understood, a drawer..."

But here I took pity on my visitor's suspense, and some perhaps on my own growing curiosity.

"There it is, sir," said I, pointing to the drawer, where it lay on the floor behind a table and still covered with the sheet.

He sprang to it, and then paused, and laid his hand upon his heart: I could hear his teeth grate with the convulsive action of his jaws; and his face was so ghastly to see that I grew alarmed both for his life and reason.

"Compose yourself," said I.

He turned a dreadful smile to me, and as if with the decision of despair, plucked away the sheet. At sight of the contents, he uttered one loud sob of such immense relief that I sat petrified. And the next moment, in a voice that was already fairly well under control, "Have you a graduated glass?" he asked.

I rose from my place with something of an effort and gave him what he asked.

He thanked me with a smiling nod, measured out a few minims of the red tincture and added one of the powders. The mixture, which was at first of a reddish hue, began, in proportion as the crystals melted, to brighten in colour, to effervesce audibly, and to throw off small fumes of vapour. Suddenly and at the same moment, the ebullition ceased and the compound changed to a dark purple, which faded again more slowly to a watery green. My visitor, who had watched these metamorphoses with a keen eye, smiled, set down the glass upon the table, and then turned and looked upon me with an air of scrutiny.

"And now," said he, "to settle what remains. Will you be wise? will you be guided? will you suffer me to take this glass in my hand and to go forth from your house without further parley? or has the greed of curiosity too much command of you? Think before you answer, for it shall be done as you decide. As you decide, you shall be left as you were before, and neither richer nor wiser, unless the sense of service rendered to a man in mortal distress may be counted as a kind of riches of the soul. Or, if you shall so prefer to choose, a new province of knowledge and new avenues to fame and power shall be laid open to you, here, in this room, upon the instant; and your sight shall be blasted by a prodigy to stagger the unbelief of Satan."

"Sir," said I, affecting a coolness that I was far from truly possessing, "you speak enigmas, and you will perhaps not wonder that I hear you with no very strong impression of belief. But I have gone too far in the way of inexplicable services to pause before I see the end."

"It is well," replied my visitor. "Lanyon, you remember your vows: what follows is under the seal of our profession. And now, you who have so long been bound to the most narrow and material views, you who have denied the virtue of transcendental medicine, you who have derided your superiors—behold!"

He put the glass to his lips and drank at one gulp. A cry followed; he reeled, staggered, clutched at the table and held on, staring with injected eyes, gasping with open mouth; and as I looked there came, I thought, a change—he seemed to swell—his face became suddenly black and the features seemed to melt and alter—and the next moment, I had sprung to my feet and leaped back against the wall, my arms raised to shield me from that prodigy, my mind submerged in terror.

"O God!" I screamed, and "O God!" again and again; for there before my eyes—pale and shaken, and half fainting, and groping before him with his hands, like a man restored from death—there stood Henry Jekyll!

What he told me in the next hour, I cannot bring my mind to set on paper. I saw what I saw, I heard what I heard, and my soul sickened at it; and yet now when that sight has faded from my eyes, I ask myself if I believe it, and I cannot answer. My life is shaken to its roots; sleep has left me; the deadliest terror sits by me at all hours of the day and night; and I feel that my days are numbered, and that I must die; and yet I shall die incredulous. As for the moral turpitude that man unveiled to me, even with tears of penitence, I cannot, even in memory, dwell on it without a start of horror. I will say but one thing, Utterson, and that (if you can bring your mind to credit it) will be more than enough. The creature who crept into my house that night was, on Jekyll's own confession, known by the name of Hyde and hunted for in every corner of the land as the murderer of Carew.

HASTIE LANYON

Henry Jekyll's Full Statement of the Case

I WAS BORN IN THE YEAR 18— to a large fortune, endowed besides with excellent parts, inclined by nature to industry, fond of the respect of the wise and good among my fellowmen, and thus, as might have been supposed, with every guarantee of an honourable and distinguished future. And indeed the worst of my faults was a certain impatient gaiety of disposition, such as has made the happiness of many, but such as I found it hard to reconcile with my imperious desire to carry my head high, and wear a more than commonly grave countenance before the public. Hence it came about that I concealed my pleasures; and that when I reached years of reflection, and began to look round me and take stock of my progress and position in the world, I stood already committed to a profound duplicity of life. Many a man would have even blazoned such irregularities as I was guilty of; but from the high views that I had set before me, I regarded and hid them with an almost morbid sense of shame. It was thus rather the exacting nature of my aspirations than any particular degradation in my faults, that made me what I was, and, with even a deeper trench than in the majority of men, severed in me those provinces of good and ill which divide and compound man's dual nature. In this case, I was driven to reflect deeply and inveterately on that hard law of life, which lies at the root of religion and is one of the most plentiful springs of distress. Though so profound a double-dealer, I was in no sense a hypocrite; both sides of me were in dead earnest; I was no more myself when I laid aside restraint and plunged in shame, than when I laboured, in the eye of day, at the furtherance of knowledge or the relief of sorrow and suffering. And it chanced that the direction of my scientific studies, which led wholly towards the mystic and the transcendental, reacted and shed a strong light on this consciousness of the perennial war among my members. With every day, and from both sides of my intelligence, the moral and the intellectual, I thus drew steadily nearer to that truth, by whose partial discovery I have been doomed to such a dreadful shipwreck: that man is not truly one, but truly two. I say two, because the state of my own knowledge does not pass beyond that point. Others will follow, others will outstrip me on the same lines; and I hazard the guess that man will be ultimately known for a mere polity of multifarious, incongruous and independent denizens. I, for my part, from the nature of my life, advanced infallibly in one direction and in one direction only. It was on the moral side, and in my own person, that I learned to recognise the thorough and primitive duality of man; I saw that, of the two natures that contended in the field of my consciousness, even if I could rightly be said to be either, it was only because I was radically both; and from an early date, even before the course of my scientific discoveries had begun to suggest the most naked possibility of such a miracle, I had learned to dwell with pleasure, as a beloved daydream, on the thought of the separation of these elements. If each, I told myself, could be housed in separate identities, life would be relieved of all that was unbearable; the unjust might go his way, delivered from the aspirations and remorse of his more upright twin; and the just could walk steadfastly and securely on his upward path, doing the good things in which he found his pleasure, and no longer exposed to disgrace and penitence by the hands of this extraneous evil. It was the curse of mankind that these incongruous faggots were thus bound together—that in the agonised womb of consciousness, these polar twins should be continuously struggling. How, then were they dissociated?

I was so far in my reflections when, as I have said, a side light began to shine upon the subject from the laboratory table. I began to perceive more deeply than it has ever yet been stated, the trembling immateriality, the mist-like transience, of this seemingly so solid body in which we walk attired. Certain agents I found to have the power to shake and pluck back that fleshly vestment, even as a wind might toss the curtains of a pavilion. For two good reasons, I will not enter deeply into this scientific branch of my confession. First, because I have been made to learn that the doom and burthen of our life is bound for ever on man's shoulders, and when the attempt is made to cast it off, it but returns upon us with more unfamiliar and more awful pressure. Second, because, as my narrative will make, alas! too evident, my discoveries were incomplete. Enough then, that I not only recognised my natural body from the mere aura and effulgence of certain of the powers that made up my spirit, but managed to compound a drug by which these powers should be dethroned from their supremacy, and a second form and countenance substituted, none the less natural to me because they were the expression, and bore the stamp of lower elements in my soul.

I hesitated long before I put this theory to the test of practice. I knew well that I risked death; for any drug that so potently controlled and shook the very fortress of identity, might, by the least scruple of an overdose or at the least inopportunity in the moment of exhibition, utterly blot out that immaterial tabernacle which I looked to it to change. But the temptation of a discovery so singular and profound at last overcame the suggestions of alarm. I had long since prepared my tincture; I purchased at once, from a firm of wholesale chemists, a large quantity of a particular salt which I knew, from my experiments, to be the last ingredient required; and late one accursed night, I compounded the elements, watched them boil and smoke together in the glass, and when the ebullition had subsided, with a strong glow of courage, drank off the potion.

The most racking pangs succeeded: a grinding in the bones, deadly nausea, and a horror of the spirit that cannot be exceeded at the hour of birth or death. Then these agonies began swiftly to subside, and I came to myself as if out of a great sickness. There was something strange in my sensations, something indescribably new and, from its very novelty, incredibly sweet. I felt younger, lighter, happier in body; within I was conscious of a heady recklessness, a current of disordered sensual images running like a millrace in my fancy, a solution of the bonds of obligation, an unknown but not an innocent freedom of the soul. I knew myself, at the first breath of this new life, to be more wicked, tenfold more wicked, sold a slave to my original evil; and the thought, in that moment, braced and delighted me like wine. I stretched out my hands, exulting in the freshness of these sensations; and in the act, I was suddenly aware that I had lost in stature.

There was no mirror, at that date, in my room; that which stands beside me as I write, was brought there later on and for the very purpose of these transformations. The night however, was far gone into the morning—the morning, black as it was, was nearly ripe for the conception of the day—the inmates of my house were locked in the most rigorous hours of slumber; and I determined, flushed as I was with hope and triumph, to venture in my new shape as far as to my bedroom. I crossed the yard, wherein the constellations looked down upon me, I could have thought, with wonder, the first creature of that sort that their unsleeping vigilance had yet disclosed to them; I stole through the corridors, a stranger in my own house; and coming to my room, I saw for the first time the appearance of Edward Hyde.

I must here speak by theory alone, saying not that which I know, but that which I suppose to be most probable. The evil side of my nature, to which I had now transferred the stamping efficacy, was less robust and less developed than the good which I had just deposed. Again, in the course of my life, which had been, after all, nine tenths a life of effort, virtue and control, it had been much less exercised and much less exhausted. And hence, as I think, it came about that Edward Hyde was so much smaller, slighter and younger than Henry Jekyll. Even as good shone upon the countenance of the one, evil was written broadly and plainly on the face of the other. Evil besides (which I must still believe to be the lethal side of man) had left on that body an imprint of deformity and decay. And yet when I looked upon that ugly idol in the glass, I was conscious of no repugnance, rather of a leap of welcome. This, too, was myself. It seemed natural and human. In my eyes it bore a livelier image of the spirit, it seemed more express and single, than the imperfect and divided countenance I had been hitherto accustomed to call mine. And in so far I was doubtless right. I have observed that when I wore the semblance of Edward Hyde, none could come near to me at first without a visible misgiving of the flesh. This, as I take it, was because all human beings, as we meet them, are commingled out of good and evil: and Edward Hyde, alone in the ranks of mankind, was pure evil.

I lingered but a moment at the mirror: the second and conclusive experiment had yet to be attempted; it yet remained to be seen if I had lost my identity beyond redemption and must flee before daylight from a house that was no longer mine; and hurrying back to my cabinet, I once more prepared and drank the cup, once more suffered the pangs of dissolution, and came to myself once more with the character, the stature and the face of Henry Jekyll.

That night I had come to the fatal cross-roads. Had I approached my discovery in a more noble spirit, had I risked the experiment while under the empire of generous or pious aspirations, all must have been otherwise, and from these agonies of death and birth, I would have come forth an angel instead of a fiend. The drug had no discriminating action; it was neither diabolical nor divine; it but shook the doors of the prison-house of my disposition; and like the captives of Philippi, that which stood within ran forth. At that time my virtue slumbered; my evil, kept awake by ambition, was alert and swift to seize the occasion; and the thing that was projected was Edward Hyde. Hence, although I had now two characters as well as two appearances, one was wholly evil, and the other was still the old Henry Jekyll, that incongruous compound of whose reformation and improvement I had already learned to despair. The movement was thus wholly toward the worse.

Even at that time, I had not conquered my aversions to the dryness of a life of study. I would still be merrily disposed at times; and as my pleasures were (to say the least) undignified, and I was not only well known and highly considered, but growing towards the elderly man, this incoherency of my life was daily growing more unwelcome. It was on this side that my new power tempted me until I fell in slavery. I had but to drink the cup, to doff at once the body of the noted professor, and to assume, like a thick cloak, that of Edward Hyde. I smiled at the notion; it seemed to me at the time to be humorous; and I made my preparations with the most studious care. I took and furnished that house in Soho, to which Hyde was tracked by the police; and engaged as a housekeeper a creature whom I knew well to be silent and unscrupulous. On the other side, I announced to my servants that a Mr. Hyde (whom I described) was to have full liberty and power about my house in the square; and to parry mishaps, I even called and made myself a familiar object, in my second character. I next drew up that will to which you so much objected; so that if anything befell me in the person of Dr. Jekyll, I could enter on that of Edward Hyde without pecuniary loss. And thus fortified, as I supposed, on every side, I began to profit by the strange immunities of my position.

Men have before hired bravos to transact their crimes, while their own person and reputation sat under shelter. I was the first that ever did so for his pleasures. I was the first that could plod in the public eye with a load of genial respectability, and in a moment, like a schoolboy, strip off these lendings and spring headlong into the sea of liberty. But for me, in my impenetrable mantle, the safely was complete. Think of it—I did not even exist! Let me but escape into my laboratory door, give me but a second or two to mix and swallow the draught that I had always standing ready; and whatever he had done, Edward Hyde would pass away like the stain of breath upon a mirror; and there in his stead, quietly at home, trimming the midnight lamp in his study, a man who could afford to laugh at suspicion, would be Henry Jekyll.

The pleasures which I made haste to seek in my disguise were, as I have said, undignified; I would scarce use a harder term. But in the hands of Edward Hyde, they soon began to turn toward the monstrous. When I would come back from these excursions, I was often plunged into a kind of wonder at my vicarious depravity. This familiar that I called out of my own soul, and sent forth alone to do his good pleasure, was a being inherently malign and villainous; his every act and thought centered on self; drinking pleasure with bestial avidity from any degree of torture to another; relentless like a man of stone. Henry Jekyll stood at times aghast before the acts of Edward Hyde; but the situation was apart from ordinary laws, and insidiously relaxed the grasp of conscience. It was Hyde, after all, and Hyde alone, that was guilty. Jekyll was no worse; he woke again to his good qualities seemingly unimpaired; he would even make haste, where it was possible, to undo the evil done by Hyde. And thus his conscience slumbered.

Into the details of the infamy at which I thus connived (for even now I can scarce grant that I committed it) I have no design of entering; I mean but to point out the warnings and the successive steps with which my chastisement approached. I met with one accident which, as it brought on no consequence, I shall no more than mention. An act of cruelty to a child aroused against me the anger of a passer-by, whom I recognised the other day in the person of your kinsman; the doctor and the child's family joined him; there were moments when I feared for my life; and at last, in order to pacify their too just resentment, Edward Hyde had to bring them to the door, and pay them in a cheque drawn in the name of Henry Jekyll. But this danger was easily eliminated from the future, by opening an account at another bank in the name of Edward Hyde himself; and when, by sloping my own hand backward, I had supplied my double with a signature, I thought I sat beyond the reach of fate.

Some two months before the murder of Sir Danvers, I had been out for one of my adventures, had returned at a late hour, and woke the next day in bed with somewhat odd sensations. It was in vain I looked about me; in vain I saw the decent furniture and tall proportions of my room in the square; in vain that I recognised the pattern of the bed curtains and the design of the mahogany frame; something still kept insisting that I was not where I was, that I had not wakened where I seemed to be, but in the little room in Soho where I was accustomed to sleep in the body of Edward Hyde. I smiled to myself, and in my psychological way, began lazily to inquire into the elements of this illusion, occasionally, even as I did so, dropping back into a comfortable morning doze. I was still so engaged when, in one of my more wakeful moments, my eyes fell upon my hand. Now the hand of Henry Jekyll (as you have often remarked) was professional in shape and size: it was large, firm, white and comely. But the hand which I now saw, clearly enough, in the yellow light of a mid-London morning, lying half shut on the bedclothes, was lean, corded, knuckly, of a dusky pallor and thickly shaded with a swart growth of hair. It was the hand of Edward Hyde.

I must have stared upon it for near half a minute, sunk as I was in the mere stupidity of wonder, before terror woke up in my breast as sudden and startling as the crash of cymbals; and bounding from my bed I rushed to the mirror. At the sight that met my eyes, my blood was changed into something exquisitely thin and icy. Yes, I had gone to bed Henry Jekyll; I had awakened Edward Hyde. How was this to be explained? I asked myself; and then, with another bound of terror—how was it to be remedied? It was well on in the morning; the servants were up; all my drugs were in the cabinet—a long journey down two pairs of stairs, through the back passage, across the open court and through the anatomical theatre, from where I was then standing horror-struck. It might indeed be possible to cover my face; but of what use was that, when I was unable to conceal the alteration in my stature? And then with an overpowering sweetness of relief, it came back upon my mind that the servants were already used to the coming and going of my second self. I had soon dressed, as well as I was able, in clothes of my own size: had soon passed through the house, where Bradshaw stared and drew back at seeing Mr. Hyde at such an hour and in such a strange array; and ten minutes later, Dr. Jekyll had returned to his own shape and was sitting down, with a darkened brow, to make a feint of breakfasting.

Small indeed was my appetite. This inexplicable incident, this reversal of my previous experience, seemed, like the Babylonian finger on the wall, to be spelling out the letters of my judgment; and I began to reflect more seriously than ever before on the issues and possibilities of my double existence. That part of me which I had the power of projecting, had lately been much exercised and nourished; it had seemed to me of late as though the body of Edward Hyde had grown in stature, as though (when I wore that form) I were conscious of a more generous tide of blood; and I began to spy a danger that, if this were much prolonged, the balance of my nature might be permanently overthrown, the power of voluntary change be forfeited, and the character of Edward Hyde become irrevocably mine. The power of the drug had not been always equally displayed. Once, very early in my career, it had totally failed me; since then I had been obliged on more than one occasion to double, and once, with infinite risk of death, to treble the amount; and these rare uncertainties had cast hitherto the sole shadow on my contentment.

Now, however, and in the light of that morning's accident, I was led to remark that whereas, in the beginning, the difficulty had been to throw off the body of Jekyll, it had of late gradually but decidedly transferred itself to the other side. All things therefore seemed to point to this; that I was slowly losing hold of my original and better self, and becoming slowly incorporated with my second and worse.

Between these two, I now felt I had to choose. My two natures had memory in common, but all other faculties were most unequally shared between them. Jekyll (who was composite) now with the most sensitive apprehensions, now with a greedy gusto, projected and shared in the pleasures and adventures of Hyde; but Hyde was indifferent to Jekyll, or but remembered him as the mountain bandit remembers the cavern in which he conceals himself from pursuit. Jekyll had more than a father's interest; Hyde had more than a son's indifference. To cast in my lot with Jekyll, was to die to those appetites which I had long secretly indulged and had of late begun to pamper. To cast it in with Hyde, was to die to a thousand interests and aspirations, and to become, at a blow and forever, despised and friendless. The bargain might appear unequal; but there was still another consideration in the scales; for while Jekyll would suffer smartingly in the fires of abstinence, Hyde would be not even conscious of all that he had lost. Strange as my circumstances were, the terms of this debate are as old and commonplace as man; much the same inducements and alarms cast the die for any tempted and trembling sinner; and it fell out with me, as it falls with so vast a majority of my fellows, that I chose the better part and was found wanting in the strength to keep to it.

Yes, I preferred the elderly and discontented doctor, surrounded by friends and cherishing honest hopes; and bade a resolute farewell to the liberty, the comparative youth, the light step, leaping impulses and secret pleasures, that I had enjoyed in the disguise of Hyde. I made this choice perhaps with some unconscious reservation, for I neither gave up the house in Soho, nor destroyed the clothes of Edward Hyde, which still lay ready in my cabinet. For two months, however, I was true to my determination; for two months, I led a life of such severity as I had never before attained to, and enjoyed the compensations of an approving conscience. But time began at last to obliterate the freshness of my alarm; the praises of conscience began to grow into a thing of course; I began to be tortured with throes and longings, as of Hyde struggling after freedom; and at last, in an hour of moral weakness, I once again compounded and swallowed the transforming draught.

I do not suppose that, when a drunkard reasons with himself upon his vice, he is once out of five hundred times affected by the dangers that he runs through his brutish, physical insensibility; neither had I, long as I had considered my position, made enough allowance for the complete moral insensibility and insensate readiness to evil, which were the leading characters of Edward Hyde. Yet it was by these that I was punished. My devil had been long caged; he came out roaring. I was conscious, even when I took the draught, of a more unbridled, a more furious propensity to ill. It must have been this, I suppose, that stirred in my soul that tempest of impatience with which I listened to the civilities of my unhappy victim; I declare, at least, before God, no man morally sane could have been guilty of that crime upon so pitiful a provocation; and that I struck in no more reasonable spirit than that in which a sick child may break a plaything. But I had voluntarily stripped myself of all those balancing instincts by which even the worst of us continues to walk with some degree of steadiness among temptations; and in my case, to be tempted, however slightly, was to fall.

Instantly the spirit of hell awoke in me and raged. With a transport of glee, I mauled the unresisting body, tasting delight from every blow; and it was not till weariness had begun to succeed, that I was suddenly, in the top fit of my delirium, struck through the heart by a cold thrill of terror. A mist dispersed; I saw my life to be forfeit; and fled from the scene of these excesses, at once glorying and trembling, my lust of evil gratified and stimulated, my love of life screwed to the topmost peg. I ran to the house in Soho, and (to make assurance doubly sure) destroyed my papers; thence I set out through the lamplit streets, in the same divided ecstasy of mind, gloating on my crime, light-headedly devising others in the future, and yet still hastening and still hearkening in my wake for the steps of the avenger. Hyde had a song upon his lips as he compounded the draught, and as he drank it, pledged the dead man.

The pangs of transformation had not done tearing him, before Henry Jekyll, with streaming tears of gratitude and remorse, had fallen upon his knees and lifted his clasped hands to God. The veil of self-indulgence was rent from head to foot. I saw my life as a whole: I followed it up from the days of childhood, when I had walked with my father's hand, and through the self-denying toils of my professional life, to arrive again and again, with the same sense of unreality, at the damned horrors of the evening. I could have screamed aloud;

I sought with tears and prayers to smother down the crowd of hideous images and sounds with which my memory swarmed against me; and still, between the petitions, the ugly face of my iniquity stared into my soul.

As the acuteness of this remorse began to die away, it was succeeded by a sense of joy. The problem of my conduct was solved. Hyde was thenceforth impossible; whether I would or not, I was now confined to the better part of my existence; and O, how I rejoiced to think of it! with what willing humility I embraced anew the restrictions of natural life! with what sincere renunciation I locked the door by which I had so often gone and come, and ground the key under my heel!

The next day, came the news that the murder had been overlooked, that the guilt of Hyde was patent to the world, and that the victim was a man high in public estimation. It was not only a crime, it had been a tragic folly. I think I was glad to know it; I think I was glad to have my better impulses thus buttressed and guarded by the terrors of the scaffold. Jekyll was now my city of refuge; let but Hyde peep out an instant, and the hands of all men would be raised to take and slay him.

I resolved in my future conduct to redeem the past; and I can say with honesty that my resolve was fruitful of some good. You know yourself how earnestly, in the last months of the last year, I laboured to relieve suffering; you know that much was done for others, and that the days passed quietly, almost happily for myself. Nor can I truly say that I wearied of this beneficent and innocent life; I think instead that I daily enjoyed it more completely; but I was still cursed with my duality of purpose; and as the first edge of my penitence wore off, the lower side of me, so long indulged, so recently chained down, began to growl for licence. Not that I dreamed of resuscitating Hyde; the bare idea of that would startle me to frenzy: no, it was in my own person that I was once more tempted to trifle with my conscience; and it was as an ordinary secret sinner that I at last fell before the assaults of temptation.

There comes an end to all things; the most capacious measure is filled at last; and this brief condescension to my evil finally destroyed the balance of my soul. And yet I was not alarmed; the fall seemed natural, like a return to the old days before I had made my discovery. It was a fine, clear, January day, wet under foot where the frost had melted, but cloudless overhead; and the Regent's Park was full of winter chirrupings and sweet with spring odours. I sat in the sun on a bench; the animal within me licking the chops of memory; the spiritual side a little drowsed, promising subsequent penitence, but not yet moved to begin. After all, I reflected, I was like my neighbours; and then I smiled, comparing myself with other men, comparing my active good-will with the lazy cruelty of their neglect.

And at the very moment of that vainglorious thought, a qualm came over me, a horrid nausea and the most deadly shuddering. These passed away, and left me faint; and then as in its turn faintness subsided, I began to be aware of a change in the temper of my thoughts, a greater boldness, a contempt of danger, a solution of the bonds of obligation. I looked down; my clothes hung formlessly on my shrunken limbs; the hand that lay on my knee was corded and hairy. I was once more Edward Hyde. A moment before I had been safe of all men's respect, wealthy, beloved—the cloth laying for me in the dining-room at home; and now I was the common quarry of mankind, hunted, houseless, a known murderer, thrall to the gallows.

My reason wavered, but it did not fail me utterly. I have more than once observed that in my second character, my faculties seemed sharpened to a point and my spirits more tensely elastic; thus it came about that, where Jekyll perhaps might have succumbed, Hyde rose to the importance of the moment. My drugs were in one of the presses of my cabinet; how was I to reach them? That was the problem that (crushing my temples in my hands) I set myself to solve. The laboratory door I had closed. If I sought to enter by the house, my own servants would consign me to the gallows. I saw I must employ another hand, and thought of Lanyon. How was he to be reached? how persuaded? Supposing that I escaped capture in the streets, how was I to make my way into his presence? and how should I, an unknown and displeasing visitor, prevail on the famous physician to rifle the study of his colleague, Dr. Jekyll? Then I remembered that of my original character, one part remained to me: I could write my own hand; and once I had conceived that kindling spark, the way that I must follow became lighted up from end to end.

Thereupon, I arranged my clothes as best I could, and summoning a passing hansom, drove to a hotel in Portland Street, the name of which I chanced to remember. At my appearance (which was indeed comical enough, however tragic a fate these garments covered) the driver could not conceal his mirth. I gnashed my teeth upon him with a gust of devilish fury; and the smile withered from his face—happily for him—yet more happily for myself, for in another instant I had certainly dragged him from his perch. At the inn, as I entered, I looked about me with so black a countenance as made the attendants tremble; not a look did they exchange in my presence; but obsequiously took my orders, led me to a private room, and brought me wherewithal to write. Hyde in danger of his life was a creature new to me; shaken with inordinate anger, strung to the pitch of murder, lusting to inflict pain. Yet the creature was astute; mastered his fury with a great effort of the will; composed his two important letters, one to Lanyon and one to Poole; and that he might receive actual evidence of their being posted, sent them out with directions that they should be registered. Thenceforward, he sat all day over the fire in the private room, gnawing his nails; there he dined, sitting alone with his fears, the waiter visibly quailing before his eye; and thence, when the night was fully come, he set forth in the corner of a closed cab, and was driven to and fro about the streets of the city. He, I say—I cannot say, I. That child of Hell had nothing human; nothing lived in him but fear and hatred. And when at last, thinking the driver had begun to grow suspicious, he discharged the cab and ventured on foot, attired in his misfitting clothes, an object marked out for observation, into the midst of the nocturnal passengers, these two base passions raged within him like a tempest. He walked fast, hunted by his fears, chattering to himself, skulking through the less frequented thoroughfares, counting the minutes that still divided him from midnight. Once a woman spoke to him, offering, I think, a box of lights. He smote her in the face, and she fled.

When I came to myself at Lanyon's, the horror of my old friend perhaps affected me somewhat: I do not know; it was at least but a drop in the sea to the abhorrence with which I looked back upon these hours. A change had come over me. It was no longer the fear of the gallows, it was the horror of being Hyde that racked me. I received Lanyon's condemnation partly in a dream; it was partly in a dream that I came home to my own house and got into bed. I slept after the prostration of the day, with a stringent and profound slumber which not even the nightmares that wrung me could avail to break. I awoke in the morning shaken, weakened, but refreshed. I still hated and feared the thought of the brute that slept within me, and I had not of course forgotten the appalling dangers of the day before; but I was once more at home, in my own house and close to my drugs; and gratitude for my escape shone so strong in my soul that it almost rivalled the brightness of hope.

I was stepping leisurely across the court after breakfast, drinking the chill of the air with pleasure, when I was seized again with those indescribable sensations that heralded the change; and I had but the time to gain the shelter of my cabinet, before I was once again raging and freezing with the passions of Hyde. It took on this occasion a double dose to recall me to myself; and alas! six hours after, as I sat looking sadly in the fire, the pangs returned, and the drug had to be re-administered. In short, from that day forth it seemed only by a great effort as of gymnastics, and only under the immediate stimulation of the drug, that I was able to wear the countenance of Jekyll. At all hours of the day and night, I would be taken with the premonitory shudder; above all, if I slept, or even dozed for a moment in my chair, it was always as Hyde that I awakened. Under the strain of this continually impending doom and by the sleeplessness to which I now condemned myself, ay, even beyond what I had thought possible to man, I became, in my own person, a creature eaten up and emptied by fever, languidly weak both in body and mind, and solely occupied by one thought: the horror of my other self.

But when I slept, or when the virtue of the medicine wore off, I would leap almost without transition (for the pangs of transformation grew daily less marked) into the possession of a fancy brimming with images of terror, a soul boiling with causeless hatreds, and a body that seemed not strong enough to contain the raging energies of life. The powers of Hyde seemed to have grown with the sickliness of Jekyll. And certainly the hate that now divided them was equal on each side. With Jekyll, it was a thing of vital instinct. He had now seen the full deformity of that creature that shared with him some of the phenomena of consciousness, and was co-heir with him to death: and beyond these links of community, which in themselves made the most poignant part of his distress, he thought of Hyde, for all his energy of life, as of something not only hellish but inorganic. This was the shocking thing; that the slime of the pit seemed to utter cries and voices; that the amorphous dust gesticulated and sinned; that what was dead, and had no shape, should usurp the offices of life. And this again, that that insurgent horror was knit to him closer than a wife, closer than an eye; lay caged in his flesh, where he heard it mutter and felt it struggle to be born; and at every hour of weakness, and in the confidence of slumber, prevailed against him, and deposed him out of life.

The hatred of Hyde for Jekyll was of a different order. His terror of the gallows drove him continually to commit temporary suicide, and return to his subordinate station of a part instead of a person; but he loathed the necessity, he loathed the despondency into which Jekyll was now fallen, and he resented the dislike with which he was himself regarded. Hence the ape-like tricks that he would play me, scrawling in my own hand blasphemies on the pages of my books, burning the letters and destroying the portrait of my father; and indeed, had it not been for his fear of death, he would long ago have ruined himself in order to involve me in the ruin. But his love of life is wonderful; I go further: I, who sicken and freeze at the mere thought of him, when I recall the abjection and passion of this attachment, and when I know how he fears my power to cut him off by suicide, I find it in my heart to pity him.

It is useless, and the time awfully fails me, to prolong this description; no one has ever suffered such torments, let that suffice; and yet even to these, habit brought—no, not alleviation—but a certain callousness of soul, a certain acquiescence of despair; and my punishment might have gone on for years, but for the last calamity which has now fallen, and which has finally severed me from my own face and nature. My provision of the salt, which had never been renewed since the date of the first experiment, began to run low. I sent out for a fresh supply and mixed the draught; the ebullition followed, and the first change of colour, not the second; I drank it and it was without efficiency. You will learn from Poole how I have had London ransacked; it was in vain; and I am now persuaded that my first supply was impure, and that it was that unknown impurity which lent efficacy to the draught.

About a week has passed, and I am now finishing this statement under the influence of the last of the old powders. This, then, is the last time, short of a miracle, that Henry Jekyll can think his own thoughts or see his own face (now how sadly altered!) in the glass. Nor must I delay too long to bring my writing to an end; for if my narrative has hitherto escaped destruction, it has been by a combination of great prudence and great good luck. Should the throes of change take me in the act of writing it, Hyde will tear it in pieces; but if some time shall have elapsed after I have laid it by, his wonderful selfishness and circumscription to the moment will probably save it once again from the action of his ape-like spite. And indeed the doom that is closing on us both has already changed and crushed him. Half an hour from now, when I shall again and forever reindue that hated personality, I know how I shall sit shuddering and weeping in my chair, or continue, with the most strained and fearstruck ecstasy of listening, to pace up and down this room (my last earthly refuge) and give ear to every sound of menace.

Will Hyde die upon the scaffold? or will he find courage to release himself at the last moment? God knows; I am careless; this is my true hour of death, and what is to follow concerns another than myself. Here then, as I lay down the pen and proceed to seal up my confession, I bring the life of that unhappy Henry Jekyll to an end.

About the Author

Robert Louis Stevenson was born November 13, 1850, in Edinburgh, Scotland. Having no interest in the family business of lighthouse engineering, he studied law, though by the time he was called to the bar, he had already begun writing seriously and never actually practiced law. Throughout his life he was often abroad, usually for health reasons, and his journeys led to some of his early writing. Best known for his novels *Treasure Island*, *Kidnapped*, and *Strange Case of Dr. Jekyll and Mr. Hyde*, he died suddenly on December 3, 1894.